COASTAL BREEZE

BY
ED ROBINSON

For fans of the original Trawler Trash Breeze;
He's back!

PRELUDE

(REPRODUCED FROM NEW RIVER BREEZE)

Brody was headed out to the porch one day when the shooting began. The glass in the door shattered and she went down. Our attacker was down by the creek, spraying automatic weapons fire into the cabin. When I got to her, I found a hole in her chest that was sucking air. I knew that to be very bad. I ripped off my shirt and wadded it up over the wound. The shooting stopped, and I heard the man running up the hill towards the back of the house, his boots crunching on the gravel driveway. I put Brody's hand on the shirt and pressed it down.

"Hold this tight," I said.

Her eyes were far away, but she was still breathing.

"Know how much I love you," I said, kissing her on the forehead.

If I stayed there with her, I'd be dead within a few minutes. My survival instinct took over. I grabbed a pistol out of the bedroom and scrambled up the stairs to the loft. Bullets blasted through the glass in the back door, which was at ground level. I got down on the floor and pointed my weapon between the wooden rail banisters, waiting for the shooter to appear. Red woke from his nap and trotted to the kitchen to see what was going on. If I called him, I'd give away my position. I heard the back door open, and Red started growling at the intruder. He was shot down instantly.

Everything that I loved was being taken from me right before my eyes. I'd felt fear before, and somehow always managed to keep my cool. The fear fought with my rage over what I had witnessed. I tried desperately to remain calm and keep my aim steady. I saw the barrel of a rifle first, and then the shooter himself. I maintained a steady aim as I pulled off five shots, directed at the man's chest. He dropped to the floor, his weapon clattering on the hardwood. I stayed where I was, watching his body for a minute. I was prepared to fire again at the slightest twitch. He was less than twenty feet away, and all my rounds had hit him.

Finally, I climbed down, keeping an eye on him. I gave a quick glance at Brody and didn't like what I saw. Red's blood was pooling on the kitchen floor. I stood over the man, pointing my gun at him. Then I saw the vest. Did my bullets penetrate it? He opened his eyes and looked up at me. I shot him in the forehead. He would never look at anything again. I didn't know who he was, and I didn't care. I only cared that he was dead.

Brody was gone by the time I returned to her. I worked on her like an army field medic, but it was fruitless. I prayed for a miracle, but it didn't come. I cursed the very God that I had just prayed to. I sat on the floor with my head in my hands, trying to comprehend what had just happened. I couldn't think. I knew that I needed to call the police, though. Instead of dialing 911, I called Rominger.

"Shooter came to the house," I told him. "He killed Brody. I killed him. Red's dead too. Send in the troops, but there's no hurry. No one left alive but me."

"Jesus Christ, Breeze," he said. "Are you hurt? Do you need an ambulance?"

"Hurts like hell, man," I said. "But not from bullets. Just get here as fast as you can."

"On my way," he said. "Hang in there."

I threw my phone through the open back door into the driveway. I picked up Brody's phone and took it outside too. I proceeded to smash them both into tiny bits. I carried our computer out back and shot it until I was out of bullets. I went back to Brody and sat with her until the first cop car showed up. An officer I didn't know came in with his weapon drawn. I put my hands up.

"I'm not armed," I said. "My weapon is there on the counter. It's empty."

He holstered his gun and took a look around.

"You Breeze?" he asked. "Are you hurt?"

"I'm not wounded," I said. "Can I get up?"

"Try not to touch anything," he said. "We'll get the detectives up here shortly."

"I'm going to go outside," I announced.

"You're going to have to sit in my car until we get some more people on scene," he said. "Sorry, procedure."

He led me by the arm to the back seat of his patrol car. He shut the door after I sat down. I knew I couldn't open that door, and it gave me claustrophobia. I started to sweat, and I couldn't unclench my teeth. Both of my fists were balled up as tight as they could get. I tried to loosen them, but they kept closing tight again. Rominger arrived and rescued me. I walked him through the scene and explained how it all went down. He wouldn't let me move Brody or Red until the detectives got a look.

They showed up and asked a hundred questions and took a hundred pictures. The only question I couldn't answer was who the guy was. Rominger and I told them about my beef with Cody Banner, and how I had killed him. We also discussed the former Banner Elk Police Chief. The shooter could have been a friend or relative of either. I knew but, didn't discuss the fact, that he could have come from Florida, or been hired by someone from my past. Either way, my location was known. I'd never be safe here. I knew I was going to have to leave.

One of them tilted the shooter on his side. The back of his skull had been blown to bits. There was a jagged hole in the floorboard where my .40 caliber bullet had lodged. They extracted it and placed it in an evidence bag. An ambulance pulled up, and his body was hauled out. I lifted Red from the floor and carried him to the back yard. A second ambulance came for Brody. I stood in the driveway trembling as they wheeled her out. I stopped them and went to her side. I pulled the sheet down from her face, kissing her one last time.

"I'm sorry, baby," I whispered to her. "I'm so sorry."

They loaded her in the ambulance and drove away. Rominger stood in front of me with his head down.

"I don't know what to say, brother," he said. "You can come stay at our place if you want."

"I don't think so," I said. "I've got a lot of work to do here."

"I can get a crew here to clean up," he said.

"That would be great," I said. "Not sure I can do it."

"I'm on it," he said. "Anything else you need, just ask."

He pulled out his phone to make a call. I went to the garage and got a shovel. I worked at digging a hole for Red for an hour. I hit solid rock three feet down. I got his favorite blanket and wrapped him up before gently placing him in the hole. After he was covered, I carried rocks from the edge of the creek and covered his grave. I couldn't have any predators digging him up. I worked like a soulless robot, trying not to replay the day's events in my mind. The cleaning crew arrived, and I showed them what they needed to do.

My closest neighbor came by to find out what had happened. We'd purchased the cabin from him. He was the one who'd built it. He offered to get the windows replaced the next day. I accepted.

"What are you going to do?" he asked.

"I don't know," I said. "You want to buy a cabin?"

"We could probably come to some agreement," he said.

"I'll let you know."

Eventually, everyone left, and I was alone. I had orders not to leave town, but no one was keeping tabs on me. The blood and gore had been erased, and the broken glass had been swept up. Thin plastic had been taped where glass used to be. It was deadly quiet, except for the ever-present hum of the creek. I stood in the middle of the cabin and let the tears come. The complete realization that Brody was gone forever hit me so hard that I thought I'd collapse. In one day, it had all come to an end. Life in the mountains had turned on us in an instant, leaving nothing but death.

Suddenly I hated that cabin. There was nothing left in it for me. I couldn't stay there that night. I grabbed some water and left, passing by Red's grave and up the hill to the woods. I walked long and hard until I reached the plateau. I watched the sun go down over Banner Elk, completely alone in the world. I spent the night in Pop's cave, lying in the dark mourning my loss. No image of the old man came to offer me wisdom. I had no dreams that gave me hope. I'd never been more alone.

In the morning I hiked quickly back down the mountain. I went to the neighbor's place with my bank account information in hand. He offered me something less than what I had paid for the cabin, but I didn't care. I took it and asked him to wire the money to my account. He said the glass company would be there later in the day. I suggested that the bill would be his, as it would soon be his house. He produced a power of attorney which I signed.

I drove into town and stopped in the local funeral home. It was Brody's desire to be cremated. She wanted her ashes poured over a waterfall that was close to our home. It was her favorite spot in the mountains. We'd been there several times in the course of our missions, but she liked to return on our free time. She would just sit and watch. It was a peaceful place.

"Can you or someone take her ashes there and fulfill her final wishes?" I asked.

"That's generally left up to the family," he said.

"She didn't have any family, except me, and I can't stick around," I said. "I've got my reasons. I'll give you five hundred extra to make sure it's done right."

"I'm sure something can be arranged."

I went back to the cabin and started packing. The first thing I did was round up all of our weapons and put them in the car. The second thing I collected was all of the cash that we had stashed in various hidey holes throughout the house. I put it in a pillowcase and stuffed it into my backpack. I put some clothes and toiletries in a separate bag. I still had room in the car, but there was nothing else I wanted or needed.

I walked through the cabin one last time, swatting away memories that threatened to make me cry again. As I looked out over the creek, I remembered my fishing rod. I found it and added it to the small load in the car. Before getting into the driver's seat, I stood in the driveway and took one last look around.

Adios, High Country. Breeze is in the wind.

ONE

I drove east to the North Carolina Coast. I couldn't think during the drive. I fought against images of Brody's dead body and Red in a pool of blood. My feelings of loss fought with my anger as emotion overrode rational thought. I found myself on Bogue Banks Island. I found a parking spot near the fishing pier and drank a beer at *Surf's Up*. I walked out onto the pier and stood amongst the fishermen. The sea breeze and the sound of the surf washed over me. I didn't know where I was going, but at that moment, I felt I needed to return to the water.

I was mad. I was mad at the shooter and whoever had sent him. I was mad at myself too. I was partially to blame. I had abandoned the one thing that had kept me alive through so many dangerous times. I'd lost my ever-present sense of awareness. I'd quit staying alert to all possible dangers at all times, and it had cost

Brody her life. I'd settled into domestic tranquility, working jobs and doing my best to be a good partner, but I had failed in my most basic duty, which was keeping us both alive.

I was also furious with God, or the Cosmic Magician, or whoever the hell was running this rock. I had made a serious effort to atone for my sins. I started working with the law instead of against it. I saved small children who were lost in the woods. I had brought justice when no one else would. I honestly tried to balance the karma scales back in my favor. All it brought me was death and heartache. Karma could kiss my ass as far as I was concerned. It was all a bunch of bullshit.

I went back to the bar and drank a few more beers. Before leaving, I ordered a shot of rum. I slammed it down and felt the familiar warmth trickle down my throat. I drove back to the bridge that would take me to the mainland. I pulled off the side of the road and watched the sun go down over Swansboro. It signaled the end of another episode in my life. I was being forced to begin anew, but I had no clue where to turn next.

My first instinct had been to run. I couldn't stay in the cabin, and I certainly didn't want to stick around for someone to take another crack at me. I had to get away, but now I was having second thoughts. Whoever wanted me dead had to be dealt with, but how? I didn't have the faintest clue as to my enemy's identity. Thinking was painful. I needed to numb myself, at least for a night. I grabbed a twelve-pack of beer and a bottle of rum before stopping at the Best Western in Silver Creek. The sweet young lady behind the counter insisted I give her a credit card. I insisted that I would pay cash.

"You can pay cash for the room," she said. "But we still need a card for incidental charges."

"There won't be any incidentals," I told her. "I'll put up a hundred just in case, and another hundred for you to stay quiet about it."

She chewed on the end of her pen before agreeing to my suggestion.

"Enjoy your stay," she said, tucking both bills into her bra.

I carried my liquid salvation to the room and got to work reducing it. I followed each beer with a shot until everything got fuzzy. I managed to get my shoes off before passing out on the bed with the TV still playing. I hadn't seen or heard a thing that was being shown, but it served as a distraction. Not thinking is a difficult task sometimes. The need to pee woke me a few hours later, and I didn't realize where I was. It took three more shots to get back to sleep.

I didn't feel so hot in the morning, and I found nothing appetizing about the continental breakfast the hotel offered. I needed some biscuits and gravy. I grabbed a cup of coffee and went to the counter to check out. A new girl was working. I asked if the night shift person had left anything for me. The answer was no. I was out a hundred bucks. I was also one more step away from ever trusting humanity again. It was going to be Breeze against the world from now on.

I drove back to Emerald Isle and found the Trading Post Restaurant. The sign said Southern Food. I ordered coffee and asked my waitress if they served biscuits and gravy.

"Best on the island," she said.

"I'll take it, with a side of bacon," I responded.

The second cup of coffee helped to clear my head. The food settled my stomach and stuck to my ribs. I left a fair tip and drove to the pier again. The ocean was calling me. I bought a bottle of water from the tackle shop and sat out on the end of the pier to watch the waves roll in. I ruminated over my situation. I couldn't stay in hotels every night. I knew that most wouldn't accept cash, but I didn't want to leave an electronic trail. I'd smashed our phones and shot our computer to bits. I'd left no indication to anyone where I was headed. I hadn't known myself. The only thing still connecting me to the world was the car. I needed to get rid of it. I really liked that car, but it was just a thing. I could sacrifice it without much regret, just like I'd sacrificed the cabin. The only material possession that I'd ever been strongly attached to was my old trawler.

Leap of Faith had been my entire life for a long time. Only my love for Brody could have separated me from that boat. I'd willingly made the choice, and it had been a good trade. Now it was all gone. I had no boat, and I had no Brody. I needed to decide whether to keep running or seek revenge. I got madder by the minute. The ocean should have been soothing, and it was, to some extent, but I realized that I couldn't leave Brody's death unavenged. I had to go back to Banner Elk and make someone pay.

I left the island and turned left at the first light. I drove up route 24 until I found a decent used car lot. They had a billboard that said *We Buy Cars!* I was offered twelve grand on a car that I'd purchased for twenty. Instead of taking cash, I picked out an SUV with plenty of room in the back. I was anticipating sleeping in the damn thing. I left the lot and went to Walmart to buy a sleeping bag and a pillow. I started driving east, back towards the mountains, with no particular plan in mind. I had six hours to think it over. There were plenty of places where I could park and sleep for the night in western North Carolina.

I had but two friends back there. Rominger would do what he could to help, as long as it was within the law. My intentions would disturb him. Angelina was a good cop, too, but I thought I might be able to influence her to aid my pursuits, or at least give me a place to stay. Going to her for help would inevitably lead to sexual tension. The little angel on my right shoulder told me it was a bad idea. It would be a betrayal of Brody's memory. Only a sleazebag would sleep with another woman so soon. I had followed the angel's advice for quite some time. It was the voice for good in my head that had led me down the narrow road to righteousness. I was in no mood to listen to it any longer. I waited for the little devil to appear on my left shoulder. It told me that Brody was gone, that Angelina was hot, and that only a fool would pass up the chance to have sex with her.

"She can help you get revenge," he said. "Win her over with your animal magnetism. She won't be able to resist and boom, you'll get what you need."

This imaginary conversation made me feel guilty about not dealing with Brody's ashes properly, but I'd been down that road before. When my wife Laura had died, I carried her ashes with me for years. They haunted me and played a part in me, not letting go. I never fully recovered until I finally got rid of the last of those ashes. I felt that I'd never recover from Brody's death anyway, ashes or not, but I knew that saving them would be harmful to my psyche. I was fragile, and I'd made a snap decision. There was no point in stressing over it now. What was done was done.

Angelina and I had experienced an instant mutual attraction. She made her desires clear, and I almost gave in to temptation. I mustered the will to stay faithful to Brody, and I was proud of myself. I couldn't know how Angelina would react if I showed up at her door. Would she jump at the opportunity to seduce me again, or would she recoil at any suggestion of physical contact? Would she help me figure out who tried to kill me? She wasn't shy, that much I knew. I assumed I could read her reaction right away. It couldn't hurt to stop by for old time's sake. If she sent me packing, I could sleep in the car, but without help, I had little to point me in the direction of the man I sought.

I wasn't running away; not yet. I was driving right back into the lion's den. Someone wanted me dead, and he thought I was in Banner Elk. Going back would make me a target, but there was no other way. I spent the rest of the drive wondering who it was. I had killed Cody Banner before he could finish raping Brody. He had connections to powerful people, but they had been brought to heel by the investigation into his crimes. Had one of them put a hit on me? I had brought down the former Banner Elk Chief of Police. My tactics had been dirty, and they drove the man insane. His actions had caused his death, but it had been me that ruined his life. Was there a relative or associate that wanted me dead? Did one of his officers pay an assassin to take me out?

I had also meddled in the affairs of the Beech Mountain Chief of Police. His wife turned out to be a murderer, which he was trying to cover up. I never went after him directly, but surely he had a grudge against me. I'd helped to jail a few meth-heads, but I didn't think they had the wherewithal to hire a killer. Who else had I pissed off? It took a few more hours of driving before it dawned on me. Brody and I had busted quite a few cheating husbands during our work as Creekside Investigations. These were men of means and money. Any one of them had the resources to find someone willing to shoot up our cabin and kill us in the process. Maybe that explained Brody getting shot first. The records of those cases were all on the computer that was now tiny bits of plastic that had made their way to a landfill by now.

I started listing the men in my head as I drove west on I-40. I knew where they lived and where they worked, but I couldn't be sure I had them all committed to memory. I recalled the demeanor of as many of them as I could. Who had the capacity to seek revenge on me? Who would know where to find a hitman? It was hard to say. I needed more information about the man I'd shot in the forehead. Who was he? Surely the cops knew by now. That's where I would start. If I knew who he was, I could look for connections to the men I'd investigated. Something would turn up, or not.

TWO

Angelina would know the shooter's identity or could find out easily enough. She was where I would start. If it meant we'd end up in the sack together, then that's the way it would have to be. With no phone and no access to the internet, I needed her help. She was the only person I might be able to trust. I had erased my digital footprint. I was driving a different car. I could sneak into town and get to work without anyone knowing I was there, except Angelina.

It was late when I made it to Avery County in western North Carolina. Angelina lived near Newland, so I didn't have to drive anywhere near the cabin, but I wasn't quite ready to show up at her door. I was weary, and my mind wasn't sharp. I pulled into the parking lot for the Profile Trail at the base of Grandfather Mountain. Hikers and campers often left their cars overnight, but the lot was empty when I arrived. I parked in a corner spot and made my bed in the rear cargo area. I was too tired to worry about dinner. Sleep came quickly in spite of the less than comfortable conditions.

My dreams featured Angelina in a variety of sexy poses. I saw her in a lacy bra and panties. I saw her in a bikini at the beach. Then I saw her walking ahead of me in tight white shorts that accentuated her fine ass. We didn't have sex in these visions, but I woke up with a boner. I felt a little guilty about it as I peed behind some bushes. The morning was cool for summer, and a light drizzle fell from gray skies. I was hungry, but I was sure I looked like hell. I slapped on some deodorant and made sure my messy hair was hidden under a hat.

I got breakfast at Hickermans before heading towards Newland. There was no car in Angelina's driveway. I knocked and got no answer. I could have driven to the Sheriff's office and had them call her on the radio, but I didn't want to reveal my presence. I didn't want to sit in front of her house all day either, so I drove to the Blue Ridge Parkway and hung out by Price Lake until early in the evening.

Her car was there when I returned. It wasn't like me, but I felt a little nervous walking to her door. I could only hope that she would invite me in and maybe even let me stay. I took a deep breath and knocked. The door opened almost immediately.

"Oh my god, Breeze," she said. "I'm so sorry. Are you okay?"

"I don't know," I said. "Trying not to think about it."

"Come in," she said. "Sit down. Tell me how I can help."

"I'm homeless and in need of a shower," I told her. "We can start there."

"What do you mean, homeless?"

"I sold the cabin to my neighbor, Richard," I explained. "Just like that. My plan was to run away and never look back."

"But here you are," she said.

"I came back to find her killer," I said. "I need your help."

"We know who the shooter is," she said. "Not a local."

"Where was he from?"

"Nashville," she said.

"Any connection to Banner Elk?"

"Rominger has been looking into that," she said. "What are you thinking?"

"I think that someone hired him," I said. "Someone who wanted me dead, or both Brody and me."

"What will you do if you find out who that person is?"

"I intend to kill them."

"Breeze, you can't do that," she said with concern in her eyes. "You're still alive and free. You don't want to end up in jail for the rest of your life."

"Wasn't planning to get caught."

"You're not thinking straight," she said. "Probably still in shock. You just need some time."

"What I need is a shower."

"Sure," she said. "Help yourself. You can stay here if you want. I'll make up a bed in the spare room."

"You're an angel," I said. "I apologize for the intrusion, but I really had nowhere else to go."

"Nonsense," she said. "I'm happy to help. Just don't go off killing anyone, okay?"

"We'll see."

She was still in her police uniform, but that didn't hide her attractiveness. I was a filthy mess. She gave no indication that she wanted to jump my dirty bones. I got some necessities out of the car and stood under the hot water for a long time. Her bathroom smelled very feminine. An array of potions and lotions stood like soldiers on the shower shelf. Her soap was of the moisturizing variety and smelled like lavender. After shaving, I slapped some smell good stuff of my own on my face. I was slightly disappointed that the lady of the house didn't try to join me while I showered.

I found her in the kitchen wearing dainty shorts and an oversized T-shirt. Her hair was down; flowing like silk. She could have passed for a college girl, preparing for a pillow fight in the dorm.

"You hungry?" she asked.

"I could eat."

"Lean Cuisine or salad?" she asked.

"Both if that's okay."

"I'll pick up some man food tomorrow," she said.

"I can do it while you're at work," I offered. "If you don't mind me staying here."

"To be honest," she began. "I'm happy to see you. Rominger said you had disappeared. Weren't answering your phone. We didn't know what happened to you."

"I smashed the phones and shot up the computer," I said. "I ditched our car far away from here. I'm incognito, and I'd like to keep it that way."

"I'm honored that you've revealed yourself to me," she said.

I thought I saw a certain look in her eyes. It could have been the first concession to the attraction that we had previously shared. It could have also been pity for the poor widower with no place else to go.

"Something told me that I could count on you," I said.

"You have good instincts."

"Can you see what Rominger has found out so far?" I asked. "I need something to go on."

"I'll check with him tomorrow," she said. "Sit down and talk to me, Breeze. Tell me what's going on inside your head."

I wasn't enthused about telling her my innermost thoughts. I hadn't dealt with them properly myself. I did know that I felt awfully alone. I told myself that it would be nice to have someone to hold, but the truth was I could use someone to hold me. I sat down on the couch and asked if she had any booze. She offered wine, which I accepted.

"You came here for a reason," she said. "Try to explain it to me."

"I came here for revenge."

"Not Avery County," she said. "To my house. I'm not talking about your crusade. I'm talking about you and me."

I hesitated before responding. My first reason was to get her help finding Brody's killer, but it had evolved from there. We had a connection; one that had never been consummated. This was the absolute worst circumstance to revisit that, but there I was.

"I hoped that you would take me in," I began. "I have no one in this world now. I'm not suggesting that we get naked and make mad monkey love. I'm asking you to be my friend."

"I am your friend," she said. "I care about you, and I'm worried about you. My heart breaks for you, and if I can ease your pain in any way, well, I'm here for you."

She moved a little closer, and I put my glass of wine on the coffee table. She opened her arms to me. I looked into her eyes and saw compassion. I accepted her hug and didn't want to let go. I put my head on her shoulder as the tears started to come. The full realization of what had happened finally caught up to me. I could no longer suppress my grief. She squeezed me a little tighter as I sobbed.

"I'm so sorry, Breeze," she whispered. "It's okay. You're going to be okay."

"I'm the sorry one," I said. "I didn't protect her. Now I'm blubbering to you like a damn fool."

"Rominger said your whole place was shot to hell," she said. "There was nothing you could have done. It's not your fault."

"I wasn't on my toes," I said. "I got lazy. I should have known."

"You're not Superman," she said. "You'll let this guilt go sooner or later. It was not your fault."

"I put us in a position where someone wanted us dead."

"Brody was with you every step of the way," she said. "She was no hothouse flower. She was your willing partner."

"She was good, Angelina," I said. "Not just competent. She was a good person."

"And I know for a fact that you loved her very much," she said, grinning slyly. "First-hand knowledge."

My mind flashed back to an earlier time. Angelina and I attacked each other passionately. I was so hard I thought I would burst. She was undoing my pants before I came to my senses. I gently eased away and kindly begged for mercy. She graciously let me off the hook. I had stayed true to the woman I loved, which earned me her respect. The two women became friends, and I suspected that they spoke of that day at some point. Brody never mentioned it, but I think she respected me even more as a result.

Now Brody was gone forever, and I was sitting on a couch with the lovely Angelina, but I was certainly in no mood for lovemaking.

"I would like to add that you are a wonderful person yourself," I said. "I appreciate you putting up with me."

"Don't be silly," she said. "I know you're hurting. I'm your friend first and foremost."

"Thanks," I said. "Do you mind if I go to my room now? I'm done talking for the day."

"Of course I don't mind," she said. "I'm sure you could use a little alone time."

"I'm good at being alone," I said. "Too good, but it will be nice to know that you're in the other room. I really appreciate this."

"Happy to help."

The sheets and comforter smelled like flowers. They engulfed me in pleasantness and made me feel safe. I was in the home of a cop, a quite sexy one, but a cop nonetheless. I drifted off to sleep with no more tragic thoughts and slept deeply. When I woke up, Angelina was gone. I'd slept until almost ten. I checked the fridge but found yogurt, fruit, and juices. I went to the coffee maker and found a note. *Just turn it on. It's all ready to go.*

I flipped the switch and brushed my teeth while waiting for it to brew. I poured a cup and wandered around Angelina's house. I resisted the urge to check out her underwear drawer or to snoop any place else where I didn't belong. She had pictures on the wall in the hallway of her various adventures. One was her in a bikini on a boat in the Keys. I swear I saw Holly in the background. Could it be? I couldn't wait to ask her about it. Holly and I had been off and on lovers for a few years and had shared quite a few adventures together. Now I stood in a house in the mountains of North Carolina seeing her in a picture with my hostess. The world couldn't be that small, or could it?

After my second cup, I was hungry. I wasn't about to eat yogurt for breakfast. I drove into Newland and found Kaye's Kitchen on the main drag. My omelet was huge and full of good stuff. My waitress was friendly and right on time. The place had an old-fashioned country feel to it. Miss Kaye herself stopped by to make sure everything was up to par. I left a nice tip and went out the door full and satisfied. I got in my car and realized that I had no place to go. I had no leads to work. I didn't want to hang out in public too much. I wasn't sure what to do next. I drove back to Angelina's and sat in a quiet house all alone. When grief tried to creep back in, I replaced it with anger. I found a notebook and a pen and started writing down as many names as I could remember from our cheating spouses cases. I added a neighborhood or street name to each, along with a description of the man involved.

When I'd exhausted my memory, I went back over the list. I added place of employment, clubs or bars frequented, and anything else I could think of. I sat and stared at my list of suspects. Nothing jumped out at me. I didn't know these men. I couldn't judge whether or not they had the balls to pay for a hit. Some of them were powerful businessmen, but that wasn't much to go on. I needed more information. Who had a connection to Nashville? I went to Angelina's computer and turned it on. It was not password protected. This was another opportunity to snoop on her history and behavior, but again, I resisted. She trusted me enough to leave me alone in her house. There was no point in spoiling that. I started searching for anything about the men on my list. It was a slow process. I thought that Brody could have done it a lot faster and better. As soon as that thought went through my mind, the overwhelming feeling of loss returned.

It snuck up behind me and smacked me on the head, almost dropping me to my knees. I cursed myself for being weak. I reminded myself of my mission to avenge her death. I tried any number of methods to stay strong, but none of them worked. I turned off the computer and went outside. I looked for any distraction, before remembering I was supposed to buy some food. I remembered seeing an Ingles Market next to the Dollar General, so back to town I went. Driving and shopping helped to take my mind off the things I didn't want to think about.

I filled my basket with meat, potatoes, and beer. I grabbed some eggs and some good old American White bread filled with GMO wheat and stuffed with gluten. I got everything I needed except for booze. I soon learned there was no liquor store in town. I had to drive back to Banner Elk, where I found the Old Smoky whiskey that I liked. I grabbed a couple of bottles of the wine that Angelina had served too. I saw no one that I knew or that might know me.

I was two beers in when Angelina came home from work. I had my notepad with the list of possible suspects on the kitchen table, just looking at it and ruminating.

"What are you studying?" she asked.

"The men we surveilled," I told her. "It's possible that one of them put a hit on me because I ruined his fun and his marriage."

"I talked to Rominger today," she said. "He came up blank, trying to connect the shooter to Cody Banner or the ex-chief."

"And both them are dead," I said. "An assassin needs to be paid by someone."

"What have you figured out so far about these other men?"

"Very little," I admitted. "I suck at computer research."

"I can access more than Google from here," she said. "Who do you want to start with?"

I looked over the names for the tenth time. None of them jumped off the page at me. I was having a hard time connecting the names to the men. I had little or no face to face contact with any of them. I couldn't summon a gut feeling from just a name. Angelina suggested we look into social media profiles. At least I could look at a picture. She started finding those that had Facebook pages, and I watched from over her shoulder.

"Keep in mind that this is their best impression of themselves," she said. "No one's life is as great as they look on Facebook."

"How much information do people put out there?"

"Some profiles are private," she said. "So you have to be their friend to see what they post. Others are public; usually those that have something to sell. Realtors, for example."

"You seem to know your way around this stuff," I said.

"I was very active at one time," she said. "Wandering Will Adventures. That was before I took this job."

"Shit, that reminds me," I said. "Is that Holly Freeman in the picture on the sailboat?"

"How do you know her name?"

"Is that a yes?" I asked.

She went to the picture in question and took it off the wall.

"You know this person right here?" she asked, pointing at Holly.

"Intimately," I said. "I was with her recently in the Virgin Islands."

"No way."

"Yes, way," I said. "She was in an accident and needed some help."

"How do you know her?"

"Back before I met Brody we were an item for quite some time," I said.

"An item? You're old enough to be her father."

"That's one of the reasons we didn't stay together; I suppose," I said. "That and our insistence on independence."

"The world has never seemed so small," she said. "I can't believe what I'm hearing."

"How do you know her?"

"I spent some time in the Keys," she said. "We met in Boot Key Harbor and hung out a lot while I was there."

"Been there a bunch of times," I said. "I met her in the Cayman's. I needed someone to help me get back to Florida, and she signed up as crew."

"Sounds like her," she said. "I thought I was an adventurer until I met her. She's a special kind of person."

"Agreed," I said. "We tried hard to make it work. We had a lot of great times, but in the end, it wasn't meant to be."

"Is she okay now?"

"I assume so," I said. "Look her up on Facebook."

Holly's personal page was private, but we discovered her YouTube channel. There had been no updates since her accident, but we spent the next hour scanning through her many videos. One of them had over one hundred thousand views, which surprised me. She had become an internet star since we parted ways.

"Good for her," I said. "But I can't imagine having my whole life out there for the whole world to see."

"I take it you're not on Facebook," she said.

"I hate computers," I said. "Phones too. They'll be the death of us all."

"You must be the last person on Earth to think that way," she said. "You and the Amish."

"Well look what we just did," I said. "We just wasted an hour dicking around instead of what we set out to do. It's an incredible time suck."

"You're right about that," she said. "But it has its good points. The world is at our fingertips."

"I prefer to keep my world small," I said. "Easier to manage that way."

"Let me organize photos of these guys," she said. "You tell me which ones to concentrate on, and I'll run them through the internet wringer."

"I'll fix us some dinner while you work," I said. "I got you some wine too."

"You're so sweet."

"You do eat meat, don't you?" I asked.

"Lean meat."

"Then filet mignon it is," I said. "Medium rare okay?"

"Sounds delicious."

I prepped to cook while she put together a file of my cheating husbands. I scanned their faces and body posture, trying to get a feel for them. Each photo brought back memories of stalking the men until they were busted or exonerated. I ruled out all of them that we determined weren't cheating. I settled on three that gave me a suspicious feeling. We took a break to eat. Over our meal, the conversation turned back to Holly.

"I'd really like to hear more about this unlikely love affair," Angelina said.

"No offense taken, by the way," I said. "Am I old enough to be your father too?"

"Not quite," she replied. "Unless you're older than I think."

"I'm fifty-six."

"Then yes," she said. "If you started early, you could be my dad."

"Shit."

"Didn't stop Holly," she said.

"True enough," I said. "But we were always aware of the age difference. I tried to be her mentor because she was so much like me."

"I can see that," she said. "Living on a boat. Beholden to no one."

"How much did Brody tell you about my past?"

"Plenty," she said. "I was kind of jealous that she was the one to tame you."

"Oh, I'm tame now, am I?"

"Figure of speech," she said. "But you did change your entire life for her."

"That I did," I said. "I'd do it all over again too."

"Do you miss it?" she asked. "I mean living on a boat, doing whatever you damn well please?"

"I thought I didn't," I said. "But without Brody, there is no reason for me to stay here. Where else would I go?"

"So you're going back to Florida?"

"I think so," I said. "I hadn't made up my mind, but I don't know what else to do. That's the life I know."

"Brody hinted at your shady past," she said. "Wrong side of the law and all that."

"I've done my best to change my ways," I said. "Thanks to her."

"What are the chances that the shooting was ordered from Florida?"

"It's possible," I admitted. "But I've been gone a long time. I haven't thought that far ahead, but if I need to get even with someone down there, I will."

"This kind of talk concerns me," she said. "You can't kill someone for revenge. It won't bring her back."

"The motive is not to bring her back," I said. "Vengeance is mine, saith the Lord."

"You're wrong about that," she said. "Repay no one for evil. Do not avenge yourself. Vengeance belongs to the Lord. He will repay."

"No shit?"

"Romans twelve," she said.

"My scripture is a little rusty."

"Anyway, it's wrong," she said. "You need to get that thought out of your head."

"Probably not happening."

"Back to Holly," she said. "You two were actually like, lovers?"

"We thought so at the time," I said. "We dedicated ourselves to understanding the meaning of love. Spent months alone together in the Bahamas; seeking something that we never found."

"That's deep."

"I think we tried too hard," I said. "That was my fault. It was my dream to find that idyllic tropical spot and share it with a lovely lady. I attempted to force that dream to come true. Holly was itching to spread her wings and see the world. She had a sailboat, and I had a trawler. We eventually figured out that it wasn't going to last."

"Where does Brody enter the picture?"

"I was wanted by the FBI, and she was one of the agents looking for me," I said. "They didn't find me."

"Wanted for what?"

"The shooting of a lady lawyer in the Bahamas, of which I was innocent," I told her.

"Who was the guilty party?"

"Holly Freeman."

"No shit," she said. "That's a story I want to hear."

"Later," I said. "The result was that Brody had reason to take a hiatus from the Bureau. She used that time to finally track me down. Just to prove that she could."

"Why didn't she turn you in?"

"By that time I had been exonerated," I said. "My boyish charm won her over to my side."

"That part I can see," she said. "She was a lucky woman."

"No, not so lucky," I said. "She would have been better off having never met me."

"I disagree," she said. "She found what most of us never do. True love."

"She lost her life."

"She would do it all over again," said Angelina.

"Kind of you to say," I said. "But it's all beside the point now, isn't it? It's cliché, but I'd gladly take her place."

"I'm going to have to figure out how to adjust your attitude," she said. "I know it's hard, but you've got plenty to live for."

"Good luck with that."

THREE

That night in bed I thought about what Angelina had said. Maybe going after Brody's killer wasn't such a great idea. I couldn't even figure out who it was yet. I remembered my last big bout of grief after my wife died. I handled it poorly, to say the least. I completely fell apart and became incapable of dealing with the world. That's what caused me to become a fringe member of society in the first place. The choices I made back then were often the wrong ones. I'd managed to survive, but I didn't need to go back down the same road again.

Even being here with Angelina was a poor decision. I knew how she felt about me. I knew that it would be wrong for us to become intimate, but here I was; flirting with disaster. If I had any sense, I'd sneak out while she was sleeping and drive through the night towards Florida. I could start over there in familiar

ED ROBINSON

surroundings. I could put the past year in the mountains behind me. I seriously considered it, but that's not what I did.

I stared at the dark ceiling and listened for sounds of her. Somehow I knew that she was coming. It wasn't long before I heard her bedroom door squeak. The door to my room opened soon after. Her body was silhouetted by a nightlight in the hall. Her hair was down, and she was naked. I moved to one side to make room for her. She slid under the covers and pressed her body against mine. We kissed long and slow.

"Say no at any time," she whispered. "I'll go, and I will understand."

She gave me every chance fair and square. All I had to do was say no, but her skin was too soft and smooth. Her touch was electric, and her smell was intoxicating. I was but a man, after all. I put up no fight. We blended together like leather and lace. The pace of our passion accelerated quickly. I could barely believe that such a beautiful creature was giving herself to me so freely, even though I knew it would happen all along. I could call myself a bastard later. This is what I had come back for. I needed someone to hold me, to love me, and to make me feel like a man. Angelina did all those things and more.

When it was over, I started to speak, but she put one finger on my lips and shook her head no. She slid silently out of bed and out the door. I listened to her dainty little feet pad back down the hallway to her room. I should have been ashamed of myself, but instead, I was grateful for her compassion. I almost packed my things to sneak away, but I couldn't force myself to do it. I had to see her before I left. I barely slept that night.

I was up before her, so I started the coffee maker. She came out in a robe a few minutes later. Her hair was a mess. She wore no makeup, and she still had lines in her face from the pillow. None of that mattered to me. I thought she looked beautiful.

"I thought you might be gone," she said.

"Good morning," I said. "Disappointed?"

"No, I guess I just pictured you as the cowboy riding off into the sunset."

"I thought about it, to be honest with you," I said. "But I felt a proper goodbye was in order."

"You're giving up on the whole revenge idea?"

"You talked some sense into me," I said. "But I suck at goodbyes. Ask Holly."

"You don't owe me a thing, Breeze," she said. "I acted of my own free will."

"As did I," I said. "No regrets."

"Let's keep it that way," she said. "I'll think of you down there in Florida, living on a boat again."

"You're welcome to join me."

"You know that's impossible," she said. "I've got a mortgage and a career here. This is home for me now."

"What happened to Wandering Will's Adventures?" I asked. "You were a free spirit once."

She stopped in mid-stride and looked at me with a mischievous grin. I thought for a second, she was ready to leave her life behind to come with me. I was in no way prepared for that, even though I had made the offer.

"It's a romantic thought," she said. "But it can't happen. I'd be a damn fool to give up everything I've worked for."

"A reasonable response from a logical woman," I said. "I, on the other hand, don't always run my life logically. It's how I always end up in trouble, but that's just how it has to be."

"It makes you irresistible," she said. "But I can't do trouble anymore."

"Don't sweat it," I said. "I just wanted to see you in a bikini."

"You should go before I change my mind," she said.

"Yes, I should," I said. "Thank you so much, Angelina. You've been a saving angel. I will appreciate you always."

"You better."

I gathered my things and loaded them in the car. Angelina came out to kiss me goodbye. It was a long, sexy affair that made me second-think leaving.

"You know where I live, cowboy," she said. "If you ever get the notion."

"I'm going to ride the waves for a while," I said. "See where that takes me."

"Thanks for the visit," she said. "I feel better about your future now."

"Me too," I said. "Me too."

I left the High Country once again, this time taking a direct route to the west coast of

Florida. I slept that night in a rest area somewhere in Georgia. I was in no hurry. I had no home and no particular place to be. The following day I made it to Charlotte County, Florida. I still had no specific destination in mind, but I wanted to see the Gulf from a familiar place. I drove to the beach at Boca Grande and walked out onto the sand. Across the Pass, I could see Cayo Costa. I once called that island home. It had always been a place to return to where I could rest and recover from whatever ailed me.

I needed a boat to get back there again. Rest and recovery were just what I needed. I was familiar with a brokerage named Pier One Yachts in Punta Gorda. Their office was within the Fishermen's Village complex, which also was home to several restaurants. I was hungry and thirsty for a beer, so I made Punta Gorda my next stop. I walked through the mall to Harpoon Harry's, ordered conch fritters and a cold one, and looked out over Charlotte Harbor. My old trawler had taken me up and down that body of water many times. *Leap of Faith* and I had made a thousand memories together.

When I first arrived in Florida in search of a boat, I wanted something economical. I didn't have much money, and a slow, single-engine trawler was just what I needed. I could go back and forth from the Keys several times without needing to buy diesel fuel. I thought about how many times I wished I could go faster. This time, I had plenty of money. I had no idea what sort of adventures a new boat would get me into, but I wanted the ability to go fast. I wanted some creature comforts, but it was just going to be me living aboard. It didn't have to be huge, but it did need to be seaworthy.

I started thinking about sport fishermen. I'd always loved their sleek style and sea keeping abilities, but they were hell on fuel. I wondered just how much money I had. I knew that I was carrying a few hundred thousand in cash. There was also a bank account with close to a half-million, but I wasn't sure about accessing that. I knew a large withdrawal could raise the suspicion of the IRS, but I was more worried about some mystery man that wanted to kill me. If a dedicated assassin could track my phone and computer usage, couldn't he tell when I took money out of the bank, and where? I wasn't sure. I needed advice on that front. I knew a man that lived in the area who could help me with that, and any other sort of problem I confronted him with.

My old friend, mentor, and benefactor lived on a yacht in Fort Myers Beach. He was often gone, traveling the world tending to his latest business enterprise. He had more money than he could ever spend, but he couldn't stop making more. Wheeling and dealing was in his blood. It was a competitive sport for him. I'd been his friend, but I'd also worked for him quite a few times. It had been lucrative, and sometimes dangerous. I decided that paying him a visit would be in my best interest. It would be good to see him again, and maybe he could help point me in the right direction. As it stood, I didn't have a plan for the future, other than to once again escape society. There was no better way to do it than living on a boat. I could hide and I could move. I could be without neighbors but still have the mobility to get what I needed. It was something I was good at.

I had tried my best to be in love with the mountains. I enjoyed the times I'd gone alone into the wilderness to be one with nature. I developed a knack for tracking and navigating in the woods, but now that I was back in Florida, I realized how much I missed saltwater. That's where I was meant to be, living on blue water.

I walked back through the mall until I found Pier One. They had a few dozen boats posted on the windows outside their office. I stood perusing what they had to offer, but nothing jumped out at me. The image of the perfect boat that I had in mind was well out of my price range. Solid sport fishermen didn't come cheap. A new one could run in the millions. I didn't need a new one, but I didn't want a bunch of old boat problems either. *Leap of Faith* had started to suffer from oldboatitis, and it drove me nuts.

The office was closed, so I walked on. Fishermen's Village had trucked in a bunch of sand and created a little beach that looked out over the harbor. I sat in an Adirondack chair and watched the sun go down. It was so beautiful it almost made me cry. Brody and I had missed the sunsets. Our cabin in the woods gave us no view of the evening sky. The mountains blocked any line of sight all around us. Now I was back in the land of awesome sunset viewing. It felt right.

After Mother Nature's display, I drove further south to Fort Myers Beach. I parked in front of the Pink Shell Marina and Resort. The beater SUV that I'd purchased didn't fit in. I saw a black Land Rover in the lot that indicated Captain Fred might be home. I walked down to the docks and found Incognito. Her sheer size dominated the little marina. I stood on the pier and called out for Fred.

"Anybody home on this rust bucket?" I yelled.

Fred's head popped out the back door almost immediately.

"If it isn't the prodigal son returned again," he said. "How are you, and why are you alone?"

"Permission to come aboard?" I asked.

"Granted," he said. "I'm guessing you're in trouble or you wouldn't be here."

"Brody is dead," I told him. "I'm on the run again."

"On the run from whom?"

"Whoever sent her killer," I said. "He clearly wanted me dead too. Even shot my dog."

"I don't know what to say about that," he said. "Come inside. Let me get you a beer."

Captain Fred didn't drink alcohol, but he always kept a fridge full of beer and wine for guests. He was also generous with his expensive cigars if you were lucky enough to stay for dinner. I selected a Landshark and sat down in the aft deck lounge area. Fred chose a bottle of spring water. He wouldn't drink the purified kind. He'd once told me that if you put enough bleach in a glass of shit, it might be technically drinkable but it was still shit.

"What the hell happened, son?" he asked.

"Life was good," I said. "Got a little gig assisting law enforcement. Had a few run-ins with the locals. Brody and I started an investigative agency. Then one day a shooter shows up and blows the place to bits, catching Brody. He came for me, but I put him down. I had her cremated and buried the dog before I split. I destroyed phones and computers. Dumped my car and here I am."

"If you killed the shooter, why do you think someone is still after you?"

"I don't know," I said. "But the shooter had no connection to me that I could determine. I assume he was hired, so his employer is still out there."

"Any idea who that person is?"

"None, really," I said. "But I didn't spend too much time trying to unravel the mystery. I made a clean break in case there was another attempt coming."

"What if it was an old score directed from Florida?" he asked. "You've come closer to the source if it is."

"I thought about that," I said. "But there's no reason for them to think I'd come here. I want to get a boat again and disappear."

"Another trawler?"

"Actually, no," I said. "I want something fast this time. Maybe a sport fisher."

"Hatteras makes the finest," he said. "I'll talk to my man up in North Carolina."

"I can't afford a Hatteras," I said.

"What's the money situation?" he asked. "You can't have blown it all already."

"Couple hundred grand in cash," I said. "More in the bank, but I'm afraid to touch it."

"A little paranoia goes a long way," he said. "I can help with that if you've got account information."

"How?"

"We have it wired to one of my offshore accounts," he said. "I'll move it around a few times until it's safe to withdraw."

"I'll have to trust you on that," I said. "But it still won't be enough for a new Hatteras."

"Bear with me," he said. "I've got the beginnings of an idea. Let me sleep on it."

"Speaking of sleep," I began. "I've been bunking in the back of an old SUV."

"You can stay here for now," he said. "I'll be happy for the company, and you'll be safe."

"I'm always in your debt," I said. "But I appreciate it very much."

"I've got a job in mind for you," he said. "It'll keep you busy and out of harm's way."

"What do you have in mind?"

"Relax tonight," he said. "I've got to make some calls. We'll talk about it over breakfast."

"Okay by me," I said. "You're a true friend. Probably the last one I have."

"You have my most heartfelt apologies for Brody," he said. "I know you loved that girl, and she was good for you."

"I'm sorry to bring it to you, Fred," I said. "I've been a little bit lost this past week."

"Keep it together, boy," he said. "We'll get you back on your feet."

"Thanks, captain."

I was given a stateroom that rivaled any fine hotel. I took a hot shower and plopped down on the comfy bed. I was out within minutes. All I saw in my dreams was blue water. Gentle waves lapped the side of a boat. The Gulf tickled my sandy toes as I walked a shoreline. Palm trees swayed in the afternoon sea breeze. Images of blue water carried me through until morning.

In the morning, I found Fred on the back deck. He had a cup of coffee in his hand and a cigar in his mouth. It wasn't lit, but it was well-chewed. He never lit them; just like he never drank. His vice was gourmet cooking.

"Eggs Benedict and candied bacon," he said. "Here's some fresh fruit to hold you over."

"Good Morning," I said. "Coffee is all I need right now."

"Help yourself," he said. "I've got a proposition we need to discuss."

I wasn't fully awake yet. I'd slept hard and was slow to come out of my stupor. I took my cup down to the lower deck to get a better look at the passing boats. A shrimper had cleared the Matanzas Bridge and was headed out into the Gulf. By the time it rounded Bowditch Point, another one came under the bridge. The shrimpers here were actually split into two fleets. One was from Fort Myers Beach, and the other was from Aransas Pass, Texas. They fished the Gulf between each port, swapping dockage at either end. It was not a glamorous way to make a living. The men aboard those boats were the hardened type. For some, it was their last chance to earn an honest buck before they ended up in jail or rehab.

Fred corralled me when I went for my second cup of coffee. I could tell he was on a mission, and I was a captive audience. I found out soon enough what he had in mind for me.

"I snooped around some last night," he said. "There is nothing in the wind about you. I think you're safe from the sugar barons."

"I hadn't even thought of them," I said. "Good to know they aren't the ones after me."

"They don't even know who you are," he said. "If they were going to seek revenge, it would be against me."

"Have you had any trouble out of them since I left Florida?"

"Not a peep," he said. "They're too busy greasing palms in Tallahassee."

"Same as it ever was."

"Which leads me to believe your troubles originate from somewhere higher up," he said.

"How high?"

"There's a lot of heat on the FBI up in Washington," he said. "Maybe they still have some loose ends to tie up."

"You don't think they took out Brody, do you?"

"Anything is possible these days," he said. "Did they know where you were?"

"They did," I said. "We had the Deputy Director at our house."

"No shit," he said. "I thought you were done with them."

"Long story," I said. "We accepted their help, with the understanding that the ledger was clear. It's complicated."

"You live an interesting life, my friend," he said. "I guess that's why we get along so well."

"So what's this proposition?"

"On a whim, I bought a fishing boat," he said. "I had this idea that I would take some time off to chase marlin down in Panama. Hasn't worked out for me."

"So the boat is just sitting down there?"

"It's not supposed to be just sitting," he said. "I hired an American ex-pat to run charters with her, but I'm not seeing much in the way of income out of the deal."

"Where at in Panama?"

"Near Boca Chica," he said. "At the world-famous Big Game Fishing Resort."

"I don't know much about Panama."

"West Coast," he said. "Middle of the jungle but only twenty minutes from the reefs."

"What's this got to do with me?"

"I want you to go down there and see what's going on," he said. "Check up on this alleged captain. Check up on my boat."

"Look out for your investment," I said. "What if he's a total loser and has been scamming you?"

"Then I'll offer you the position," he said. "If you don't want it, I'll want you to bring the boat back to Florida."

"I'd have to go through the Panama Canal," I said.

"That's Panama City to Colon," he said. "No — big deal."

"I know diddly about marlin fishing," I admitted. "But I can handle a boat."

"That's why you're the perfect man for the job," he said. "Lucky for me, you showed up out of the blue. Plus it will get you safely off the radar."

"Until I return to Florida anyway," I said.

"This plan has a phase two," he said. "It's about your bank account."

"I'm listening."

"I won't even attempt to hide the transaction," he said. "We'll wire your money to a bank in Panama. You'll waltz right in and withdraw it. Anyone still trying to track you through electronic transactions will know where you are."

"Why is this a good idea?"

"Because you won't be there," he explained. "You'll be on a boat heading back to Florida. No exit visa, no airline ticket. They'll assume you've lost yourself in that country with a wad of cash."

"This is all assuming your captain isn't pulling his weight," I said. "What if he's legit?"

"If you want the boat, you'll take it from him whether he's truly trying or not."

"What do you mean if I want the boat?" I asked.

"The boat is yours," he said. "All you have to do is go down there and get it. You don't even have to come back here if you don't want, though I'd advise getting it far away from where it is now."

"You're kidding."

"I rarely kid," he said. "The boat is doing me no good as it is. It's costing me slip fees and a kickback to the resort. I'm also paying that knucklehead a salary. You'll be doing me a favor by taking it off my hands."

"Not to sound greedy, but what kind of a boat is it?"

"A Hatteras, of course."

"How big?" I asked.

"It's a GT54," he said. "Too nice for a boat bum like you."

"I don't deserve something like that," I said. "What's the catch?"

"I may have a need for your services from time to time," he said. "If you are going to be around Florida, I'd like to call on you when I need you."

"I was hoping to go back to Pelican Bay," I said. "I'd be an hour away in a boat like that."

"With no phone or email," he said. "Unless you still have that SAT phone I gave you a long time ago."

"I don't," I said. "To be honest with you, I didn't trust it anymore."

"Smart move," he said. "I change them up every couple of months. I'll get you a new one for your trip so you can keep me posted."

"Just like that," I said. "Fly to Panama and pick up a boat. Bring it home and live on it."

"Just like that, son," he said. "Welcome back."

FOUR

My circumstances were changing dramatically and quickly. It helped to keep my mind off Brody and Red. I'd been consciously avoiding those memories in order to cope. I showed up in a ratty old car with few possessions, but soon I'd be living large in the vessel of my dreams. It didn't seem real. I knew that Captain Fred was wealthy and generous to a fault, but I never expected anything like what he was offering. Whatever he called on me to do in the future would be my pleasure. I had nothing else to do with my life. I may as well spend it repaying his kindness. In between duties, I could float in the calm waters of Pelican Bay and waste my days chasing fish and catching rays. It looked like things were going to work out for me. Shit always works out.

Fred called the Panama Big Game Fishing Club, and they arranged my travel itinerary.

First, I was to fly into Panama City and then catch a short flight to another airport in David. The club would pick me up and transport me to Boca Chica, for a boat ride across the channel to Isla Boca Brava, where the resort sat high above the water.

"It's well-appointed," Fred told me. "They do a nice job taking care of you. Your boat is the biggest and newest in the fleet. I'll make sure that you have full rein of the facilities and complete cooperation from the club."

"Did you catch a marlin when you visited?"

"The wind howled for three days while I was there," he said. "A local guide took me inshore fishing, but that's not really my thing. I spent most of my time by the pool. They offer their own branded cigars that rival the world's finest. Seeds from Cuba, grown in Nicaragua and the Dominican by the real pros. Aged to a glorious finish and stamped with the club's logo. Those alone are worth the trip."

"I'm not much of an aficionado," I said. "Marlin fishing sounds exciting though."

"You've never caught a marlin?"

"Holly and I hooked one in the Gulf Stream once," I said. "But we broke it off."

"I don't think you're going to want to hang around long enough to go after marlin," he said. "Take care of business. As soon as you get your money from the bank, be gone."

"Are you sure the bank is going to allow me to make such a big withdrawal?"

"I've got a few million in that bank," he said. "I've already called the manager there. He'll be expecting you. It will be drawn from my funds to make him happy. Your deposit will reimburse me."

"I'm not sure how a person says thanks for a situation like this," I said. "But I'm grateful."

"What's the point of being rich if you can't spend it on your friends?" he said. "You've never asked for money from me. You've always stepped up to help whenever I needed it. I loved Brody too, and I know you're hurting. Maybe this will ease the pain somewhat."

"You're a good man, Fred Ford," I said. "I don't care what all those ladies say about you."

"Ha," he said. "I always treat the ladies well, and you know it."

"I defer to your greater experience," I said. "I'll be sticking to boats and fish for a while."

"You do have a way with boats," he said. "Never seen a man so naturally talented on the water. What's your secret?"

"You must become one with the vessel, grasshopper," I said. "Feel her and listen to her. Anticipate her response and give her what she wants."

"Just like women," he said. "Then I should be better at it."

"You care more for women than you do boats," I said. "I think I'm the other way around."

"You cared for Brody, though," he said. "You gave up your boat for her."

"I gave it my all, captain," I said. "In the end, it broke my heart. I'm trying not to let it break my spirit."

"Well, there's a new girl waiting for you down in Panama," he said. "Give her the same attention that you gave *Leap of Faith*."

"What is the new girl's name?"

"Incognito, of course," he said. "Incognito VI."

I had always called my old trawler *Miss Leap*. I knew that I'd call this new boat *Miss Six*. I wouldn't change the name that Fred had christened her with, but I could personalize it to suit my liking. It had a nice ring to it. I was anxious to get started on a new journey. This time I'd be riding in style. There were still some details to work out. Fred and I sat down that night and hashed out the rest of the logistics. I couldn't enter a foreign country carrying a ton of cash, so he gave me a credit card for fuel and incidentals. I was to return it the next time I saw him. I offered to pay him back whatever I spent, but he wouldn't have it.

"You're on my dime until you get back to Florida," he said. "After that you're on your own."

I would, however, be leaving Panama with a large amount of cash. I wouldn't be clearing customs on my way out of the country. I'd simply head offshore and never return. Anyone looking for me would think I was still there, long after I was gone. My passport and the bank transactions would indicate I had checked in. There would be no trace of my departure.

I spent some time using Fred's navigation system to get a feel for the return trip. It was a long damn way, and I'd need to refuel a few times. It was roughly seven-hundred miles to Georgetown in the Cayman Islands. That would be my stopover point. I'd been there a few times before and I was familiar with it. In fact, it was where I first met my old friend and sometimes lover, Holly. I'd also come to know a cab driver there named Theo. Maybe I could look him up.

My new boat held twelve-hundred gallons of fuel. If I didn't push her too hard, I wouldn't have any problems. I'd figure out the best running speed for time and conservation once I got underway. Working on these calculations got me excited. It had been too long since I'd been out on the open sea. It would take twenty-four hours to get to the Caymans. I could rest there and make an easier, shorter trip to the Keys the next good weather day. This would be a whole lot different than putting along at six knots like I had been used to.

Fred hooked me up with a SAT phone and showed me how to use it.

"If you need to call anyone other than me, say a marina, you'll need to put the numbers in now," he said. "It doesn't have internet capability, but it's secure."

I plugged in the numbers for the Georgetown Yacht Club in Grand Cayman, and the Key West Bight Marina. After I left Key West, it would be one easy day back to Fort Myers Beach or on to Pelican Bay. My new life would begin upon my return to the west coast of Florida. I added the number for the Coast Guard out of Key West too, just to be safe. I didn't want to deal with them if I could avoid it. They might have questions about my re-entry to the States, but in an emergency, I knew I could count on them. The homeport for *Incognito VI* was Fort Myers Beach, so I shouldn't raise any suspicions once I got inside U.S. territorial waters.

Captain Fred had a travel agent that he used often make my flight arrangements. The Big Game Club would handle the rest. Once he knew my flight times, he called them to firm up the details. He was assured that I'd be given first-class service, which would be another thing I wasn't accustomed to. I'd been a salty boat bum and a dirty mountain man, but never a wealthy traveler. Fred was hooking me up right.

He also had travel plans of his own, as he was working on some mysterious deal in Colombia. His flight was earlier than mine, so I'd have to wait a few hours at the airport bar. That didn't seem like much of an inconvenience considering the scope of the trip. The day before we were scheduled to leave, I drove my rattletrap to the Fort Lauderdale Airport and left it in long-term parking. Fred had a limo drive me back. We also took a limo to the Fort Myers airport when it was time to leave. We split up immediately upon arrival. Fred made haste to his gate while I dawdled in the parking garage deciding which bar to waste a few hours in. I paid eight bucks for one beer and grumbled about it under my breath.

"I've heard it all before," the bartender said. "I hear it's worse in the bigger airports."

"I don't get to airports much," I said. "I can buy a whole case for less than twenty dollars."

"Pack a few in your carry-on next time," he said. "Buy one and sit and drink your own after that."

"Does that work everywhere?"

"Depends on the bartender," he said. "Switch out your empties when he's not looking."

"Good tip. Thanks," I said. "Not much good at the moment, though. Hit me with another eight-dollar beer."

There were no direct flights from Fort Myers to Panama City. My Delta flight would first take me to Atlanta, where I waited another two hours before boarding a plane to Panama. That cost me twenty dollars for two more beers and made me sleepy. I napped most of the way. I only had an hour wait for the short hop to David, which gave me just enough time to visit the men's room and grab a snack. Upon landing there, I was greeted by a pretty young representative of the Big Game Club. A big, black SUV drove me to the water's edge on Boca Chica. Next to the Panama Sport Fishing Lodge was a landing where I boarded a small boat. It took me across the channel to Boca Brava and the Panama Big Game Fishing Club.

I was given a personal tour and shown to my room. I dropped off my bags and walked down to the docks. *Incognito VI* stood out amongst the fleet. She was indeed the biggest and newest boat in the harbor. The rest were Blackfins and Bertrams in the twenty-eight to thirty-one-foot range. They showed some wear, but were in good condition and tidily kept. The Hatteras was a different story. Her stainless was salt-encrusted and there were old bloodstains on the teak deck of the cockpit. Her captain wasn't showing her any love. He didn't seem to be around, so I stepped onboard for a closer look.

Fishing rods were still in the rocket launcher behind the flybridge. They too were covered in salt. The mono line was cooking in the late day sun. This dude was a lousy caretaker of some very expensive equipment. The door was locked, but I guessed that the interior was a mess as well. I walked back to the club to find the boss man. I introduced myself, and the man snapped to attention.

"Relax," I said. "This is a fine place you have here. I want to ask about Jim Starr, captain of Incognito."

"Mr. Fred told me about your mission," he said. "You have my full cooperation."

"How does this Starr fellow get away with being so lazy?"

"We would prefer to kick him out," he said. "But we don't wish to anger Mr. Fred."

"I don't like what I've seen so far," I said. "Does he catch fish? What good is he?"

"He only takes charters when he is forced to," he said. "We often get complaints. Such a shame for a beautiful boat like that."

"Will he give me trouble when I tell him why I'm here?"

"I don't think he is a violent man if that's what you're worried about," he said. "He's drunk most of the time. We wouldn't tolerate fighting here. He would be gone, Fred or no Fred."

"I'll try not to cause a ruckus," I said. "Where can I find him?"

"He plays guitar at the Tiki Bar on Boca Chica," he said. "But he sleeps on the boat."

"Do you have a small boat available that I could borrow?" I asked. "Maybe it's better if I confront him off these premises."

"They are owned by our staff," he said. "Let me see what I can do. Please, have a drink on the house."

Never one to turn down a free drink, I sidled up to the bar. I ordered a beer and was given an Atlas Golden Light. It tasted pretty much like a Bud Light and went down quickly. Before I could ask for another, the manager came with one of his employees. Guillermo wouldn't let me take his boat, but he would drive me. He was familiar with the waters, and his boss allowed him to be my driver and escort.

I was led to a small panga type vessel with an ancient outboard. Guillermo grasped the pull rope, tilted his head a certain way, held his tongue just right, and gave it a yank. The old motor fired to life with a billow of blue smoke. I sat on an overturned milk crate and turned my hat around backward.

"Let her rip, Guillermo," I said.

"Si, señor Breeze."

The little boat cut the water like a knife, and we zipped back across the channel in just a few minutes. The Tiki Bar was to the east of the way I had crossed the first time. It sat alone but within sight of a hotel. I pointed at it.

"Bocas Del Mar," Guillermo said. "No fishing."

The Tiki Bar had a long narrow dock with room for two small boats. Several sailboats were anchored off nearby. It was just like any tiki bar anywhere else on earth, complete with a thatched roof. On a barstool in the corner sat a man with a guitar. Jim Starr was singing Jimmy Buffett to four tourists drinking fruity concoctions. Tee-shirts and license plates adorned the walls and hung from the ceiling. A Nacionales beer was two bucks. I took a barstool and listened to the man with the guitar.

When he finished, I offered to buy him a drink. He gladly accepted and sat down next to me.

"You're not half-bad," I said.

"Thanks, bud," he answered.

"You make a living down here doing this?"

"Not much of one," he responded. "Some days, I drink more than I earn. Just playing for tips."

"That's too bad," I said. "Because you're about to lose your house."

"I don't have a house, man," he said. "I live on a boat over at the Big Game Club."

"Not anymore."

"Say what?" he asked.

"I'm here on behalf of the boat owner," I told him. "He told me that if I found you lacking that I was to return the boat to Florida. I find you lacking."

"You're just jerking my chain, right?"

"Not at all," I said. "The boat's a mess, and you haven't been bringing in any money. You're fired."

"I can't make money with that boat down here," he said. "Fuel costs are more than the charters run. It's impossible. Better to leave it at the dock than lose money every trip. That's why the locals all run those small boats with a single engine."

"So you thought you'd just liveaboard at the owner's expense and hang out at the tiki bar all day?" I asked. "You could have been straight with him. He's a fair man."

"He's got more money than he knows what to do with," Starr said. "I'm surprised he even remembers he bought that boat. Small change to him."

"Underestimating Captain Fred is where you went wrong," I said. "If you had talked to him, maybe he might have moved you to a more profitable location, or otherwise kept you employed. Now you're out on the street; effective immediately."

"Where am I supposed to sleep tonight?"

"Not my problem," I said. "But I'll be staying on the boat and preparing to leave with it as soon as possible. Have you kept up on her maintenance?"

"I have," he said. "That's one thing I'm good at. I've been a mechanic all my life. She's good to go other than near-empty fuel tanks."

"Can you even catch fish?"

"Anyone can catch fish down here," he said. "But I was a no-good gringo. The other captains kept me out of the loop. I'd get some tourist his first marlin. He's all happy with the trip of a lifetime until we get back to the docks and the other boats have all caught five or six bigger fish. He shorts me on the tip, and it takes a thousand bucks to fill up with diesel. That shit got old real fast."

"Sorry it didn't work out for you," I said. "Take that guitar to the city. Maybe you can make enough to survive."

"You're a cold son of a bitch," he said.

"Just doing my job," I said. "Like you should have done."

"Look, I've got no place to go," he said. "I can't sleep in the mangroves. The bugs or snakes will kill me. Let me stay aboard until I can make other arrangements."

"I'm staying aboard," I said. "I can't trust that you won't try to take me out in my sleep. Nothing personal but you're on your own."

I took a good close look at him; sizing him up. He had soft eyes and a passive posture. I didn't see an ounce of violence in the man. I did see desperation. I knew what that was like. I rethought my position and decided to cut him a small break.

"I'll talk to the manager at the club," I said. "Get you a room for a few nights. I'll put it on

Fred's tab. But you'll need to figure out something fast. I want to get out of here soon."

"Thanks, pal," he said. "That's better than nothing."

"If you so much as look at me cross-eyed the deal is off," I said. "And behave yourself until I'm gone or you'll regret it. Understood?"

"Gotcha," he said.

I put a ten-dollar bill on the bar.

"Have another beer or two," I said. "Give me time to talk to the Club. Meet me at the boat later."

FIVE

Guillermo ran me back across the channel to the Club. I talked to the manager about a room for Starr and made my way down the docks to closer inspect Incognito VI. She needed a good scrubbing inside and out. Dirty clothes were strung about the interior. Empty beer bottles and cigarette butts were scattered everywhere. Dirty dishes had attracted flies, and the trash can was overflowing. I was disgusted by the sight. No matter how poor I had been, I'd always kept my boat clean and livable. I had all the time in the world, why not keep things tidy?

I took a look in the engine room, and to my surprise, it was sparkling clean. I pulled both dipsticks, and the oil was golden. The batteries were properly watered, and the fuel filters looked good. Tools were stowed neatly, and the bilge was dry. Maybe he really was a mechanic. At least he'd taken care of that side of things. I went up on the bridge and fired the engines one at a time. They purred like happy kittens, with almost no smoke out of the exhaust. They were in tune and running smoothly.

I left them to warm up and started cleaning. I was hosing down the cockpit when Starr showed up.

"Permission to come aboard?" he asked.

"Granted," I said. "How about grabbing a scrub brush while you're here?"

"I don't work for this boat anymore," he said.

"The owner is paying for your room," I told him. "Make yourself useful."

The cleaning went faster, with an extra set of hands. We got all the grime and dust off before taking a break. I sent Starr to the bar with a bucket and orders to fill it with beer and ice. We sat on the gunnels and tried to empty all the full bottles.

"How did you get hooked up with Fred?" I asked him.

"Through a friend of a friend," he answered. "Don't blame him for hiring me. I may have embellished my resume somewhat."

"I'm surprised you were able to fool him."

"I was running a private boat for a zillionaire in the Keys," he said. "The owner's wife took a liking to me. The guy had no reason to fire me, but he wanted me out of the picture, so he gave me a glowing recommendation."

"You never did his wife?"

"Don't shit where you eat," he said. "She was doable, that's for sure, but I didn't want to spoil a good gig."

"But her attentions spoiled it for you anyway."

"Wasn't my fault," he said. "I can't help it if I'm irresistible to the lonely wives of rich men."

"So there was more than one incident?"

"I learned my lesson after the first time I lost a job," he said. "That was up in Miami, and I'm lucky the husband didn't shoot me."

"Now you'll be looking for a new avenue to grift the elderly rich."

"Fred Ford can fend for himself," he said. "There was no grifting involved."

"Until you got down here and sat on your ass doing nothing."

"The tropics are bad for a man's ambition," he said. "But there's nothing here for me now."

"What are you going to do?"

"I was hoping that I could hitch a ride back to the Keys with you," he said. "No hard feelings and bygones be bygones."

"I can run this boat," I said. "I don't need any help."

"Except for through the Panama Canal," he said. "Tough to do by yourself."

"How did you manage on the way here?"

"I hired an agent on the other side," he said. "I still had one of those Fred Ford credit cards at the time."

"Do you think the two of us can do it without hiring a local?"

"I don't see why not," he said. "Most of the lock operators speak some English. We can do it."

"Fuel stops?"

"There's a marina at the entrance," he said. "Flamenco I think it's called."

"What about on the eastern side?"

"I stopped at Club Nautico, in Colon," he said. "But that was because I needed help to get through. There's an easier stop on the other side, called Shelter Bay."

"Can we make a jump to Grand Cayman from there?"

"Can't be done," he said. "I did the math on the way down. At thirty knots it's a twenty-four-hour trip. We've got twelve hundred gallons of fuel, and she burns close to one hundred gallons per hour at that speed."

"Well, that sucks," I said. "Where did you get fuel?"

"This is why you need me," he said. "The Nicaraguan coast is all preserve with no fuel to be had, but if you slow troll up to Honduras you can get good diesel there. It's less than four hundred miles to the Caymans from there. It's still going to be tight, so you can't run her hard across there."

"What about from there to Key West?"

"We'll have to stop in Cuba," he said. "Not in Havana but on the western tip."

"I've made it a habit to avoid Cuba," I said. "I didn't know that there was a marina anywhere near there."

"Gaviota Cabo San Antonio," he said. "The only reason they have diesel is to service the Cuban Navy, but they will gladly accept private boats. They actually get paid from us."

"You're a wealth of information," I said. "But Cuba gives me the willies. My old trawler could make it from Grand Cayman to Key West without a fuel stop. Of course, I only traveled at six knots."

"It would take us four days at six knots," he said. "And we'd probably still run out of fuel."

"In a hurry?" I asked. "What's this boat burn at full slow?"

"It idles at six knots," he said. "But I never ran it that slow. I don't have an answer for you."

"If it burns ten gallons per hour and gets six knots, we can make it," I said. "Hell, we can make it thirteen or fourteen gallons per hour."

"At ten knots she burns better than twenty per hour," he said. "I don't think your figuring is going to work out."

I realized that this Hatteras was going to take some getting used to. The fuel burn was mind-boggling. The fuel capacity wasn't enough to overcome the horrible mileage. Adding extra fuel in drums or bladders wouldn't help much; not burning a hundred gallons per hour. Fortunately, this trip was being paid for by Captain Fred. I had to wonder how I'd make out when the diesel cost was on me, which reminded me that I was supposed to make a substantial withdrawal before my departure. If I took Starr with me, I'd have to worry about him wanting that money bad enough to kill for it. A guy like him might find that much money worth the risk, especially when we were alone on the high seas. It was a lot to think about. The beers weren't helping.

I decided to cut our conversation short and sleep on the topic. I sent him to a nicely appointed room at the club and prepared my defenses for the night. I had no gun, so I had to settle on a rusty filet knife for a weapon. I put a big bean bag chair on the inside of the salon door. It wouldn't stop the door from opening, but it would slow down an attacker. I tied some empty cans to the inside of the door, hoping that they would rattle enough to wake me. I would have felt much safer with my trusty old shotgun within reach.

Working on the problem took me back to a different time; a time before Brody. I once possessed a superior awareness that slowly faded away in the mountains. There was a time when my life depended on careful planning like this and being constantly vigilant. Whoever had killed Brody wasn't going to find me in Panama. If I was protecting myself from Starr then why would I consider taking him with me to Florida?

I'd lost track of how many times I'd lost everything, but I hadn't lost my sense of self-preservation. This time was different, though. I had money. I was taking possession of an expensive yacht. Was it enough to get me past the loss of the best woman I had ever known? I'd been in a state of denial since leaving the mountains. The life that I had sought for so long was over. The woman that I loved with everything I had was gone. I'd lost my purpose for living, so why was I trying so hard to stay alive?

There was one other thing that I'd been denying; someone was responsible for Brody's death. I should be seeking to avenge her instead of running away, except I didn't know where to start. There wasn't much I could do about it in Panama. I needed to get back to the States and come up with a plan. The quickest way to do that was to enlist the help of Jim Starr. If he killed me for the money, then my problems would be solved. I would no longer care about earthly problems.

I gave in to sleep, and the dream came almost immediately. Brody was with Laura, my first love. The two of them sat on a couch. A pair of teacups were on a silver platter on a table in front of them. They were engaged in deep discussion, but I couldn't hear what they were saying. My hound dog, Red, slept at Brody's feet. The only thing missing from the room was me. The two women smiled and laughed before the image faded away. I was left with a deep feeling of loneliness. Breeze was an island; alone in a vast sea of nothingness.

I was not in a pleasant mood the next morning. There was no coffee on the boat. The interior was still a wreck, and I was hungry. I walked up the dock to the bar and was immediately handed a cup of rich, dark java.

"Do you serve breakfast?" I asked the bartender.

"Inside the dining room," he said. "Very good."

"Thank you."

I went inside and saw Starr at one of the tables. I asked for bacon, eggs, and toast before sitting down with him.

"Good morning," he said.

"You can come along with me," I said. "We'll do it your way. Get me to Florida, and I'll get you to Florida."

"Thanks," he said. "I appreciate it."

"I need to make a stop in Panama City," I said.

"You'll have to get a cab from that first marina I told you about," he said. "Flamenco. The city isn't far, maybe five or six miles. What do you need there?"

"A bank."

"They're all in the same district," he said. "Which one?"

"I'll tell you when I find out," I said. "First you need to clean up your crap inside the boat. I'm going to want the sheets washed too. After that, we'll take on fuel. Where do we get groceries around here?"

"You don't," he said. "Closet decent store is in David."

"That's over an hour inland," I said.

"The club can arrange transportation," he said. "You're still in good standing. Slip the manager some cash. He'll make it happen."

"What's the deal with guns down here?"

"The laws are fairly lax, but only for legal residents," he said. "You have to get a permit first."

"That won't do," I said. "What about the black market or private sales?"

"I couldn't tell you."

"Can you find out?"

"These folks have had enough of me," he said. "No one is going to sell me a weapon."

"Then we may need to make some additional stops in the city," I said.

"Should I ask why you think you need a gun?"

"We'll be adding some additional cargo that will need to be protected," I said. "Maybe even from you."

He looked surprised and maybe even a little offended. There was a pause in the conversation while we ate. I asked for more coffee.

"Listen, pal," he began. "You show up here to take my boat, which is my only home. I need your help getting back to Florida, so I'm not holding it against you. A man's gotta do what a man's gotta do, but there's no need to hold me in contempt. You need me too. I got that rig down here, and I can get it back, without traveling at a measly six knots. We're both men. Let's work together for both our benefits."

"I've got my reasons to be wary, Starr," I said. "You'll know more when we get to Panama City. Now excuse me while I make a call."

I asked the server to put both our meals on Captain Fred's tab and walked back to the Hatteras. She really was a beautiful boat. The stainless still needed polishing, and the teak trim could use some attention, but there would be plenty of time for that later. We were about to become well acquainted. If I survived the trip, we'd be good friends by the time we got to Pelican Bay.

I dug the new SAT phone Fred had given me out of my bag.

"How's Panama treating you?" he asked. "That boat ought to be a step up for you."

"We're preparing to leave soon," I said. "Which bank am I going to?"

"We?"

"I'm letting the previous captain hitch a ride," I said. "It will make the trip easier."

"That's up to you," he said. "How did he take his dismissal?"

"I think he was expecting it," I said. "But maybe not so soon and so sudden."

"Keep them off-balance," he said. "It's a good tactic in every negotiation."

"Which bank, Fred?"

"There's a CitiBank downtown with all the other banks," he said. "It takes up a whole block between 59th and 60th. You're to see the bank manager, Rick Earles. His wife Patty is his assistant. They're Americans through and through. I've got some investments through them down there. Good people. They'll be expecting you, but don't show up looking like a boat bum. Stop and get a suit before trying to walk out of a bank with half a million dollars."

"Thanks for this," I said. "I suppose I'll be on camera during this transaction."

"That's the way you want it," he said. "If Big Brother is watching he'll see where you've been, but he won't know where you've gone to."

"Panama Breeze," I said. "I like the sound of that."

"Stay safe, my friend," he said. "See you soon."

Starr gave me a few pointers about the boat before we moved her to the fuel dock. I was cautious and careful handling the new vessel in the yacht basin. We tied up at the pumps with no difficulties. A little while later, I signed off on the four thousand dollar diesel bill. Fred was going to get that bill, as I had no credit card of my own nor nearly enough cash. I could pay him back after I got back to Fort Myers Beach if he wanted me to.

Back in the slip, I played with the GPS, plotting a course for Flamenco Island and the marina there. The trip would take close to ten hours and burn all of the diesel that we'd just taken on. That made me second-guess accepting the Hatteras as a gift. It was a boat for a wealthy man, not a boat bum like me. If I thought it wouldn't piss off my benefactor, I'd look into selling it and buying something more economical, but that was a thought for another day. My immediate mission was to return to Florida aboard the Incognito VI.

Six

The weather was good, and it was time to take off. Starr had cleaned up his mess, and I had laundered the sheets and some of my clothes. We made a run to David for supplies, including beer, but no hard stuff. The boat had minimal refrigerator space and no oven. It did have a cooktop and a microwave. It also had a washer and dryer, which I found ridiculous. I started drawing up plans in my head to remove them and stick a fridge in there, but the more I poked around, the more cold storage I found. There was an additional freezer hidden away in a cockpit compartment, as well as what Starr called a cold box. It proved perfect for beer storage.

The lines were pulled in, and I idled gently out of the slip and into the channel between the club and Boca Chica. We ran southwest along the coast, between Coiba Island and the mainland until we rounded Punta Mala. From there we turned north, passing Toboga Island heading for Panama Bay. We crossed the ship channel and dodged some ferries running back and forth before circling around Flamenco Island and going through the breakwater to the inner harbor.

It was a well-protected basin with nice floating docks and plenty of yachts fancier than ours. The dockmaster spoke fluent English while directing us to our slip. The Panama City skyline was plainly visible to our north. It was not a place I'd visit given a choice, but it was convenient to the canal and was known to sell clean diesel. After tying up, we walked up the dock to the resort, called Puerto Amador. We were served an expensive dinner on a fine linen tablecloth by a beautiful young waitress. That went on Fred's card too. At this rate, I'd be broke by the time I finished paying off my debt to him.

I grabbed some literature on the Panama City attractions on the way out. Just beyond the banking district was a shopping district. It boasted of several fine gentlemen's clothing establishments, including Oscar De La Renta,

Kenneth Cole, and Hugo Boss. I liked the looks of a place called Suit Supply Panama. I couldn't imagine ever needing to wear a suit after this trip, so there was no need to get the latest and greatest in men's fashion. I had decided to take Starr with me to the bank, as somewhat of a bodyguard. He could at least watch my back while I carried the money. That meant he needed a suit too.

It was late in the day, and I was too tired to go to town, so we retired to the boat for a few beers. I watched the sun go down over the Pacific from the fighting chair. I believe it was my first Pacific sunset. I guess you're never too old to experience new things. You have never really "seen it all." I had gotten to know my passenger a little better. He was a likable sort but had no real prospects ahead of him. He said he used to know some people in Cape Coral, and that if he could find a place to stay he'd have another boat job in no time. He didn't seem to be stressing over his lack of employment. He just drifted along waiting for the next opportunity to present itself. I guess we weren't really that different. I had no prospects either, but I didn't want any. I did have a place to live, and soon I'd have enough cash to last me as long as I was frugal.

I didn't see Starr as a threat, but I didn't have the money yet. I'd have to watch him closely for any signs of betrayal, while at the same time relying on his help. I didn't think he could fool me on the navigation front. I'd been down this far south before, picking up a boatload of coke from Cartagena. I'd plied the Rio Dulce in Guatemala and helped friends bring up some gold off the coast of Belize. I did want to get my hands on a gun though, just in case.

The resort ran a van into the city several times a day. We hitched a ride and spoke freely with the driver. Drivers always know what's going on in their city.

"Let's just say a fellow wanted to purchase a pistol," I said. "Where would one go about that?"

"Do you mean outside the legal method?" he asked.

"We aren't residents," I told him. "Just passing through. It will be out of the country in two days."

"By the casinos," he said. "Walk the block, and someone will try to sell you one. Or stop in the right bar. You will see what I mean."

"Can you take us there and wait?"

"I can park at the Crowne Plaza," he said. "One block to their casino."

"Make it so," I said, slipping him a twenty.

The walk opened my eyes to how American Panama City was. There was a McDonald's, Domino's, and a Carl's Jr. on the way. We passed several hotels, and a Budget Rent A Car before we started to see what we were looking for. Just past the DoubleTree was Le Palace, a strip club. Outside was an old fashioned hawker, calling us to see the beautiful women. I got close enough to whisper my need for a gun. He directed me to the Goldbar Lounge and told me to ask for Big Juan. We made a U-turn and found the place with no problem. It was advertised as a restaurant, but the staff was barely clothed and overly friendly. I shook a hot blonde off my arm and asked for Big Juan. She looked at me, curiously. I showed her a twenty dollar bill and said slowly, "Juan. Big Juan." She took the bill and my hand, leading me to a back room. I looked for my backup, but he was occupied by a dark-haired cutie. I was led into a dark room in the back of a bar in a foreign country. Big Juan had what amounted to a pawn shop. It was stocked with plenty of expensive watches, rings, and guns.

"It's always the Americans," he said. "I wouldn't take these pieces if I didn't know that an American would soon be by looking for one."

"Nice to meet you, Juan," I said. "I'll be out of your hair shortly. How much for this one?"

"Five hundred American," he said.

It was worth only half that, but I was a beggar and couldn't be a chooser. Juan was big, as advertised, and he wore a permanent scowl. I wanted out of there as soon as possible.

"Bullets?" I asked.

"You get whatever is in it," he said.

"May I check?"

"I'll do it for you," he said. "I will hand it to you once I get the cash."

The Glock 19 holds fifteen rounds plus one in the chamber. The chamber was empty, but the magazine was full. He removed the magazine and looked at me expectantly. I counted out the five hundred, so he could see, and we traded.

He didn't give me the magazine until I was ready to walk out the door and he made sure I'd seen the weapon he had on his person. Juan was a careful man. The blonde cutie led me back towards the exit. I had to pull Starr away from the fine young thing he was snuggled up to. She was disappointed to lose what she thought was a sure customer.

We hustled back to the Crowne to catch our driver before he lost patience with us.

"Shopping district," I said. "Suit Supply please."

"I will have to leave you then," he said. "I'll be back down here in two hours if not sooner."

"We need to get to Citibank too," I said.

"It's ten or twelve blocks if you want to walk," he said. "Plenty of cabs if not."

"Sure, thanks," I said. "Where can we wait near the bank?"

"Café Madero," he said. "It's behind Capitol Bank. You can get a coffee."

"See you in a couple of hours, my friend."

The staff of the suit store was more than happy to accommodate us. We were both able to get moderately priced attire that looked more expensive than it was. Then came the accessories. We needed shoes, socks, belts, and dress shirts. Neither of us had anything that would go with our new suits. The total bill was beyond what I wanted to spend, but we had no choice. Maybe Starr would need his to get a new job. Maybe I would attend a funeral or a wedding someday. For now, we needed to look sharp long enough to complete my bank transaction and get back to the marina in one piece.

My new dress shoes felt weird on my feet as we walked towards the banking district. It had been a very long time since I'd been dressed like a businessman. Flip flops were the only footwear I brought on this trip. I was beginning to work up a sweat as we approached the bank. We slipped inside a shop to soak up some air conditioning before proceeding. I pretended to look at the knick-knacks while Starr exchanged pleasantries in Spanglish to the clerk. I felt a touch of nervousness about what we were about to do. I was out of my element in dress clothes and banks weren't my favorite place to be. The money was worth a little discomfort, though. I took a deep breath and motioned to my partner that I was ready.

We found the building, which was completely fronted in glass. The sign said Citibank N. A. Surcusal Panama. I patted the weapon tucked into an inside pocket of my jacket and entered the lobby. There was a reception desk manned by a serious-looking gentlemen who immediately greeted us.

"We are here to see Mr. Earles," I said.

"Do you have an appointment?" he asked.

"Not specifically for today," I said. "But he is expecting us."

"Just a moment, please."

He eyed us suspiciously as he picked up a phone. He turned his back to us and put his hand over his mouth as he spoke. I tried to look professional. I had even shaved for the occasion. Finally, he hung up and turned around.

"He will see you," he said. "Please wait for an escort."

Starr and I looked at each other and shrugged. Within a minute an armed guard appeared and motioned for us to follow him. We rode the elevator to the top floor and were led to an elegant office. The guard asked us to wait outside. Starr and I shrugged again. We were soon allowed to enter, and the atmosphere changed dramatically. Earles and his wife greeted us like old friends.

"Welcome to Panama City," said Rick Earles. "This is my wife, Patty. Can I get you a drink? Anything, anything at all."

"We appreciate your hospitality," I said. "But we don't want to take up too much of your time."

"Nonsense," he said. "You obviously don't know how much Fred Ford has invested in this bank."

"Not my business," I said. "But it's nice to have friends abroad."

"Mr. Ford has instructed us to take care of your every need," he said. "Just ask, and it's yours."

"Just here for my money," I said. "Don't need anything else at the moment. Thank you, though."

"Of course," he said. "We took the liberty of placing it in a nice briefcase," he said. "How will you be transporting it today?"

"We're at the Flamenco Marina," I said. "They run a van back and forth to the city."

"Please allow me to call a car service," he said. "This is a very safe city, but it's not Mayberry if you know what I mean."

"And we're sitting ducks carrying this kind of cash?"

"It's in my best interest to see that you arrive safely at your destination," he said. "Let me get you a cold beer while you wait."

"I could go for a cold one," Starr said.

"Okay, me too," I said. "Can we see the money now?"

"Patty," said Earles. "Bring out the cash for Mr. Breeze and his friend."

We were each handed a frosty bottle of Panama Lager and offered a seat. The sofa was fine leather, and the view was quite stunning if you like a city panorama. The beer was ice cold and quite tasty. Patty returned with a sharp-looking case and opened it for my inspection. The small stacks of hundred dollar bills didn't look like much. I guess I was expecting a much bigger load to carry.

"You're welcome to count it," Earles said. "But believe me when I say that we would never try to cheat a friend of Mr. Ford's or any other customer for that matter."

"I'm sure it's all there," I said. "I'm grateful to you for helping out with this."

"My pleasure," he said. "We haven't seen Fred down here in a long time. I understand he's been working on a project in Colombia."

"I'll tell him you were asking about him," I said.

Just as we finished our beers, Patty announced that our car was ready. The guard walked with us to the curb where we were picked up by a new looking limo.

"Marina Flamenco?" the driver asked.

"Yes, please," I said. "Do you have a phone?"

"I do, sir," he said. "Do you need to make a call?"

"Please inform the marina that we won't need to be picked up," I said. "And thank you."

"It is no problem, sir."

I wasn't used to being called sir or riding in fancy limos, but it was a nice touch. It felt safer than walking to a café and waiting for a van. I knew that I'd feel even better once we got back to the boat and stashed the cash. Then my only worry would be Starr. So far he'd shown no signs of ill-intent, but I knew what that kind of money could do to a person.

As soon as we changed out of our monkey suits and stowed the money, my attention turned to the Panama Canal. Starr had done it once, but I didn't know what was involved, what it would cost, or how long it would take. I was also devising a plan to earn his loyalty, or at least prevent him from a mutiny.

SEVEN

I realized that I needed his help because I had
no idea how the process worked. I couldn't
search for answers on the internet. He had one
whole trip's worth of experience, which was a
world more than I had. He also was familiar
with the boat. I had no choice but to take him
on as crew and to rely on him to get us both
back to Florida. He'd have ample opportunity
to take me out and assume ownership of both
the boat and the money once I was out of the
picture. I decided to buy his cooperation.

"Listen up, Jim," I began. "Let's make a deal
right now. I've decided to compensate you for
your assistance."

"I'm listening."

"Five grand in cash for getting us through the
canal, and another five grand when we arrive
safely in Fort Myers Beach. I'll hand you
bundles of hundreds when you step off the boat
in Florida and split."

"I will gladly take your money," he responded. "But you didn't have to worry about me. I had no schemes to rip you off."

I put my hand out and looked him dead in the eyes. He took my hand, and we shook on the deal. He returned my stare. I saw nothing in it that hinted at a possible betrayal. I didn't even have a gut feeling that he would double-cross me; I was just playing it safe.

"So give me the rundown on the canal crossing," I said.

"We can't do it by ourselves."

"What?" I almost screamed.

"They require four line handlers," he explained. "One for each corner of the boat. You hire an agent, and he'll line up your helpers and guide you through the paperwork."

"What's that cost?"

"I had to pay each line handler a hundred bucks," he said. "Transit fee was eight hundred. There's also a measurement fee and some other piddling costs."

"Measurement fee?"

"They have to measure you to figure out your fee," he said. "But everything under fifty feet is eight hundred. Can't get out of the measuring though."

"Where do we find an agent?"

"I used a guy named Tito on the other side," he said. "Should be some info at the marina office for someone around here. You get a good agent, and he handles all the details. Then an advisor goes along with us, not the same guy. You're expected to provide meals and refreshments for the advisor."

"He'll hold our hands through the process?"

"Pretty much, but always remember that you're the captain of the vessel," he said. "Listen to his advice, but you are always in command. You have to keep an eye on the line handlers too. They'll be on their phones right when you need them most. Keep them on their toes."

"How long does it take?"

"A day or two depending on traffic and big ships," he said. "The hard part is getting permission to enter in the first place. They won't start opening locks until they have a sufficient number of boats lined up to cross."

"How long did it take you?"

"I was lucky," he said. "Only waited two days."

"I guess we better find an agent then."

"Almost forgot something," he said. "We have to get four super long lines and some tires."

"Tires?"

"They rent you these old tires with cloth and rags all wrapped around them," he said. "The nicer ones are covered in plastic, but you'll need those instead of fenders, or in addition to fenders."

"So we give everything back on the other side? Including all the men we'll have?"

"Right," he said. "You drop anchor and call for the water taxi. No biggie."

We walked up to the office, but it was closed for the day. We found the dayroom and checked out the message board on the wall. Sure enough, Tito's name was written on an index card and thumbtacked to the board. Neither of us had a phone or anything to write with so we took the card and went back to the boat. I used Fred's SAT phone to call him. I had to leave a message, which meant I had to leave the phone turned on and charged up. He didn't return our call until the next morning. I guess even Panamanian Canal agents have regular business hours.

He was quite friendly and knowledgeable; a real take-charge guy. His English was good. He got some boat information from us and our passport numbers and said he'd call us back. I hated being tied to a phone, but I had no choice. Later in the day, we heard from our advisor, who lived in Panama City. He had line handlers ready to go once we got permission to enter the canal. He drove down to inspect our boat and collect his cash in advance. Two more days went by before we heard from Tito again. The "Ad Measurer" was coming the next day to measure our boat. He'd give us forms that needed to be taken to the bank along with payment. Citibank handled these transactions on our end.

I somehow failed to realize that my new boat was well over fifty feet. The fee jumped from eight hundred to thirteen hundred in an instant. There was also something called a "Buffer Fee," which was basically a deposit. If all went well, you could get a refund once passage was complete. That was another nine-hundred bucks. The measuring guy asked for our help to hold his tape measure, but only until it was obvious that we exceeded the fifty-foot mark. He sat down in the salon to fill out his paperwork; the 4614 - Ad Measurement Clearance and Handline Inspection, 4312 - Handline Undertaking to Release and Indemnify, and the 4627 – Handline Dockage Request. I was given a form entitled "Attachment to 4614" and a Ship Identification Number to take with me to the bank.

The form requested my bank account information. It appeared that my deposit would be transferred to my account soon after completion of our passage. I was pretty sure that I no longer had a bank account, as I'd just emptied it. The deposit was nine hundred bucks. I wasn't sure it was worth the trouble, but it was still a good bit of money. We had to go to Citibank to pay our fee, so I decided to inquire once again with Rick Earles while we were there. He seemed eager to assist me the first time.

We took the van again into the city the next day. I was able to pay the upfront fees in cash. I watched while the clerk faxed my paperwork to the Panama Canal Authority. There was nothing else to do but wait. I asked to see Mr. Earles and went through the same process as the first time.

"No, I don't have an appointment," I said. "But I'm sure he'll see me."

I handed my account information to Earles and explained my dilemma. He handed it to Patty, and she left the room. We had another Panama Lager while we waited. When Patty returned, she seemed confused.

"Your account has a considerable balance, Mr. Breeze," she said.

"Just Breeze is fine."

"It's the same amount as what we gave you in cash," she said.

"Fred must have wired his own money here," I told her. "I'm certain he'll pay himself back out of my funds. He just hasn't gotten around to it yet."

"Do you mind if we verify that?" asked Rick.

"Of course not," I said, concealing my nerves.

Patty left the room once again. I nursed my beer and waited expectantly. I was called into the adjacent office and handed the phone.

"Breeze my boy," said Captain Fred. "How's Panama treating you?"

"Okay so far," I responded. "Am I okay with this transaction?"

"I had a change of heart on the paper trail," he explained. "At least until you're clear of that country. I can wire the funds to one of my accounts in any number of places. I'll take it back in good time."

"You think someone could respond so fast that they'd find me here?"

"Depends on who it is," he said. "Until we know that you can't be too careful."

"I'm glad someone in this operation has brains," I said. "We're finishing up the canal paperwork now. Hopefully, we'll be underway soon."

"Stay alert," he said. "I'm working some leads on my end, but nothing definitive yet."

"Head on a swivel, captain," I said. "Once we hit the Atlantic we shouldn't have any worries."

"Are you making out okay with your passenger?"

"I believe we've come to an understanding," I said. "Thanks again."

"I'm staying here on my Incognito until you show up."

"It's good to know you're there," I said.

We were all satisfied, so I went back downstairs to turn in the form that would allow my deposit to be returned. It was a simple thing, but it felt like a small victory at the time. Once we got back to the boat, I called Tito. He had not yet received a transit date but assured me that he would call as soon as he heard something. Jim and I had time to kill until he called.

I bought some more cleaning supplies from the marina and put my crew to work polishing stainless. I cleaned the bridge enclosure and studied the GPS route back to Florida. We filled the boat with fuel and went over our departure checklist the following day. We figured out where and how to hang our tire fenders and where to stow the long ropes. We filled the water tanks and bought some more groceries. We drank our share of beer and rum at the resort bar while we waited to hear from Tito.

He finally called and gave us a departure date for two days out. We called the advisor and he made sure our line handlers were available and ready to go. We settled our bill with the marina and waited out the next day impatiently. We called to double-check that we were still a go. Everything was set for my first, and hopefully my last, Panama Canal Crossing.

The next thing I knew there were six people on the boat, four of whom didn't speak English. Every command had to be given to the advisor who then relayed it to the line handlers. I eased Incognito out of her slip and joined the group of boats lined up just before the Bridge of The Americas. I was tuned to VHF channel 12 to hear the controller's call for us to make our way to the first lock at Miraflores. All vessels stood clear as an impressively large freighter came under the bridge after completing its passage through the canal. Then it was our turn.

I gave the order to prepare the long lines and eased the throttles forward. I was glad not to be first in line. I got to watch the boats in front of me and prepare for whatever came next. When traveling from west to east, the locks lower the water level at each stage. As the water began to recede, the lines had to be adjusted. One of the handlers didn't seem to understand this simple concept. He didn't understand my English when I yelled at him either. Starr ran to the dummy's corner and quickly loosened the rope before it got too tight and snapped. My advisor yelled at the young man in Spanish. I don't know what he said, but it sounded like a blistering rebuke.

"Good job, Jim," I yelled from the bridge. "Keep an eye on all of them."

"Aye aye, captain," he yelled back.

We repeated the process after just a few minutes in the Pedro Miguel Lock. After that, we had a good long stretch of clear sailing that brought us out into Gatun Lake. The line handlers were all napping, so the advisor went down to nudge them awake and prepare them for the Gatun Lock.

"You will anchor in Limon Bay," he said. "I'll show you where. The water taxi can take us with the lines and fenders to shore. It is best that you don't visit Colon. It is not a safe city for foreigners."

"I'll take your advice," I said. "I assume I can trust you to return the ropes and fenders."

"If I do not, I would no longer be hired for these trips," he explained. "I make sure they get to the proper place."

"Do I pay each guy individually or can I give it all to you?"

"You can pay me the total," he said. "I will distribute it accordingly."

The last lock was the easiest as the line handlers seemed to have figured out how the process worked. Neither Starr nor the advisor had to reprimand any of them. There were long breakwaters at the mouth of Limon Bay, but I could feel the power of the ocean beyond them. We jockeyed amongst the boats we'd been traveling with for a good anchoring spot off the city of Colon. Soon several taxis appeared, and I was unburdened of my Panamanian crew. They seemed to appreciate the crisp hundred dollars bills they'd been given.

"Why didn't you tell me how much was involved in this deal in the first place?" I asked Starr.

"I don't know," he began. "If you thought you needed me, you were more likely to agree to take me back with you, or something like that."

"Because once I had an advisor, I wouldn't need you at all," I said.

"Now, you know."

"We have a deal now," I said. "Let's try to be straight with each other, okay?"

"You're right," he said.

"Now point me to the marina," I said. "It's beer-thirty."

Shelter Bay Marina was much nicer than I expected. I don't know how the rest of the country is for living conditions, but this was the second nice marina I'd seen. The floating docks were nice and the slips plenty wide. They had all the amenities of any American marina, but I soon learned that they all came with a price. If you wanted WIFI, it was ten dollars per day. A shower was five dollars, and use of the pool was another five. I also learned that we could have brought our crew directly here, and the marina would return them and all the gear for twenty-five dollars. It would have saved us some time and hassle.

The place was filled mostly with American and Canadian cruising boats, predominantly sail. Our trip through the canal had taken nine hours, so we were just in time for happy hour at the bar. No one was headed north. Some were bound for the Pacific, but most were staying put. It was cheap enough for cruisers to stay for an extended period, or even use as a home away from home. The downside was it was far from anything on land. A bus ran into Colon for shopping needs, promising "safe delivery." It was fenced and manned by security guards at night. We decided to order food and listen to some good old conversations in English.

"What are you going to do back in Florida?" I asked Starr.

"With a little money to get started on, I'll try to find a cheap place to rent," he said. "I'll mingle and work my way into something eventually."

"Have you thought about playing in the bars there?"

"I don't think I'm good enough for that," he said. "Lots of competition."

"I hear guys with guitars all the time that can't carry a tune," I said. "Coconut Petes, I call them. Singing about boats without ever having been on one."

"Lots of bars in Fort Myers Beach," he said. "I suppose I could give it a go. Call myself Panama Pete."

"I know a guy that plays at the bar right next to the dinghy dock," I said. "I'll introduce you. Maybe he can help you out."

I was referring to Scott Bryan, but I was really thinking about a pretty bartender named Jennifer. It had been years since I'd been in there. There was a good chance neither of them were still around. I had a brief mental picture of

Jennifer and me going at it at her place. It only happened once, but it was a good memory. I could walk there from the Pink Shell, where Fred's boat was docked. It was a little something to look forward to. I had to be careful about looking back. Brody was in that direction.

After drinking some personality, Jim Starr started working the crowd. I knew what he was up to. He was looking for a yacht that needed a captain or a mate, but sailors are a cheap lot, and he wouldn't find any takers. He'd be better off in Miami or Fort Lauderdale for that kind of scam. He was likable enough, but his game was too transparent. I still couldn't understand how he'd bamboozled Captain Fred. Myself, I played it straight. I was what I was, and I avoided pretending to be someone else. My pitch had always been - take me or leave me for what I am. It had served me fairly well with Fred and with the ladies.

I left Starr to work the room and took a bottle of Ron Abuelo aged rum back to the boat. It was surprisingly smooth and tasty. I sat at the helm and looked over our route to Florida. I didn't like the multiple fuel stops in sketchy places, but there was nothing I could do about it. I had someone to watch my back, and I also had a gun. The canal crossing had been the tricky part. Now, all we had to do was not run out of diesel between Panama and Key West. How did I keep finding myself in these adventures? They had become the essence of me, temporarily interrupted by my time in the mountains. I had immediately fallen back into the ways of the sea; almost like I'd never left. I was destined to forever remain a boat bum.

EIGHT

I decided to call Captain Fred to give him an update now that we were free of the locks. It felt as if I'd hardly been in Florida at all. I wanted to get back there and begin my new life harassing fish and soaking up the sun. I also wondered if he knew anything about the identity of Brody's killer.

"We're at a marina inside the break wall at Limon Bay," I told Fred. "If the weather cooperates we can be there in four or five days."

"Scratch that," he said. "I'm going to have to detour you."

"Detour?" I asked, "To where?"

"You ever been to Cartagena?"

"As a matter of fact, I have," I said. "It was a dangerous place when I was there."

"If you were hauling drugs, of course it was dangerous," he said. "You'll be staying in a nice and safe marina near the center of tourism. Should be no problem."

"Why am I going to Cartagena?"

"I need a message delivered to a certain politician there," he said. "Right up your alley."

"So call him up," I suggested.

"Not that kind of message," he said. "Something a bit more intimidating."

"You want me to rough up a politician?" I asked. "In Colombia? Why?"

"He's the last man standing in the way of an important deal," he said.

"What the hell are you up to?"

"Have you heard of China's Belt and Road Initiative?" he asked.

"Not even remotely."

"The Chinese have been throwing money at underdeveloped countries to enhance infrastructure," he began. "There is interest involved, of course. An influence to peddle."

"What's this got to do with Colombia?"

"I'm emulating their efforts, albeit on a smaller scale," he said.

"You're lending the government money for roads and bridges?"

"And influence," he said. "I've got big plans for the future. Once they owe me a few hundred million, those plans will slide through the process and make me billions."

"Don't you already have billions?"

"I couldn't pull this off if I didn't," he said. "I've been laying the groundwork for this for years. Now one asshole is threatening to derail the whole operation."

"I don't know anything about their government," I said. "But how does one guy have so much pull?"

"He represents the district that encompasses Cartagena," he said. "It's the second most important area outside Bogota. He also leads the Green Alliance Party."

"So his beef is environmental?"

"The environment, social justice, and economic sustainability," he said. "You'd have to understand how the government works down there. They based it on our system, but there are over twenty parties. The president's party only holds thirty-five seats out of one hundred and sixty-six. He's got to get the lesser parties to go along with whatever he wants to do. It usually involves bribery."

"So why don't you bribe this guy?"

"You're going to try that first," he said.

"First?"

"You'll need to stick around to make sure he follows through on his promise," he said.

"And if he doesn't?"

"You'll put the fear of Fred in him."

"You know I still have the previous captain of this vessel with me, right?" I asked.

"You may need him," he said. "Have you two been getting along?"

"We're fine," I said. "But I doubt he'll be happy about the detour."

"He doesn't have much choice, does he?"

"He's at the bar trying to worm in with the yachties," I said. "But not having much luck."

"Put him on a plane if you have to," he said. "But I need you in Colombia soon."

"You're the boss," I said. "I'll take care of it."

"Leave the phone on," he instructed.

I didn't want to put Starr on a plane. I wanted him to help me get home. I didn't want to go to Colombia either, but it looked as if I'd sold my soul for a big, new Hatteras. It was time to pay the piper. I'd never turned down Fred before. He'd been more than good to me. He'd been incredibly generous. I had to do what he asked. Starr would have to come along for the ride, whether he liked it or not.

On my previous trip to Cartagena, I had two armed men to assist me. They came in handy. The harbor had an ominous feel to it, like all hell could break loose at any minute. I was not in a fancy marina, though. I had anchored off the industrial area to accept my load of cocaine. Street thugs knew what was going on, and when I went for fuel, they thought they might relieve me of some of my cargo. Diver Dan and Robin had not hesitated to show their firepower and discourage any attempt at boarding. I didn't think Starr had those kind of balls, and he did not have a weapon of his own. We were going to have to have a talk about my new mission after he sobered up.

Speaking of sober, my alcohol stream had a little too much blood in it. I had an expensive bottle of fine rum that would fix the problem. I suspended any worries about the upcoming detour and devoted my energy to lessening my sobriety. I had a lot of catching up to do after quitting the hard stuff in the mountains. I drank it straight and warm. Sophisticated types call that "neat." I was not a sophisticated drinker. I didn't even use a glass.

Good quality rum reduces the severity of hangovers, so I was okay in the morning. Starr had stumbled in sometime after I'd gone to bed and was still asleep. I went out on deck to take in the salty ocean air. I wondered how far it was to Cartagena. I went up on the bridge and powered up the GPS. The trip was three hundred miles as the crow flies, well within our fuel range at thirty knots. I'd have a little bit of reserve, so I could push the throttles forward and see what she could do, for a brief time.

When Starr got up, I broke the news to him before he was fully awake.

"Coffee?" he asked.

"Cartagena," I said. "We gotta go there."

"What the hell for?"

"Doing Captain Fred a favor," I said. "It's three hundred miles. We can be there in ten hours."

"Coffee first," he said. "Fucking Cartagena?"

We walked up to the restaurant and got breakfast, with lots of coffee. When Starr was more coherent, I told him about my mission, hoping to make it our mission.

"I need a weapon," he said. "And a cut of whatever he's paying you."

"He's paying me with this boat," I said. "I'm doing him a favor, for free."

"So I'm an unpaid co-conspirator?"

"You're getting ten grand to be on this trip," I told him. "This is just a little detour from what we originally agreed to."

"Colombia is not a country to be fucking around in," he said. "And I'm no secret agent. Why would you even consider such a thing?"

"Because I already owed Fred before he gave me this boat," I said. "If he needs me, I'm there for him. It's why he trusts me and takes care of me. You could learn a little something from that."

"So you've done this kind of thing before?"

"I've been shot at in the Bahamas and chased by a helicopter off the coast of Cuba," I said. "Fred had one of his boats blown to bits in Fort Myers Beach, but I wasn't on it at the time. I kidnapped his daughter from an unworthy boyfriend and brought her back against her will. I have not, however, strong-armed a politician in a third-world country."

"There must be more to Fred Ford than I realized," he said.

"He last sponsored me and a team of mercenaries to drain Lake Okeechobee onto the sugar cane fields," I said. "He's not afraid to get his hands dirty to further his goals. I'm occasionally one of his tools. It's a good partnership."

"Until you get killed so he can make some more money," Starr said.

"I've got nothing better to do and nothing else to lose," I said. "I'm going, with or without you."

"Screw it," he said. "Give me a day to clear my head and see if I can scare up a weapon. I'll go."

"Best bet is to look for a boat from Texas," I suggested. "Skip the Canadians altogether."

I went to the office to get a weather report while Starr roamed the docks. He'd made himself familiar with most of the cruisers the previous night, so he wasn't out of place. I learned that the Caribbean Sea was forecast to be calm for several days, which was great news. I could only hope for similar conditions when it was time to escape Cartagena. Back on the boat, I played around with distances to alternate destinations. Jamaica was too far. I had no interest in a fuel stop in Venezuela. The only good option was to hug the coast of Costa Rica and Nicaragua until we could make it to Grand Cayman. Florida was only getting farther away.

Starr returned with a Smith and Wesson revolver and a box of extra rounds. It was the 686 model which fired the .357 caliber round. It felt heavy when I hefted it, and the stainless steel finish was nice.

"We're going to need some oil to keep these things from rusting," Starr said. "A cleaning kit too if we ever have to use them."

"God forbid," I said. "Only if our lives are in the balance."

"I've never shot anybody," he said. "Have you?"

I had, but I didn't want to get into it with him. Some bad hombres had shot up *Leap of Faith* with me onboard back in Pelican Bay. When they came around for another pass, I peppered them with my shotgun. It was light shot, and the guy didn't die, but it was enough to get them off my ass. I was loading bales of weed from a shrimper near the Dry Tortugas along with Diver Dan and Robin when we were approached by an unmarked boat with no lights but lots of horsepower. All three of us unloaded our weapons at the men on board. It was doubtful that anyone survived. Up in the mountains, I'd shot Cody Banner through the back with a high-powered hunting rifle before he could complete his rape of Brody, and most recently dispatched Brody's killer with a close-up and personal shot to the head. So the answer was yes, but Starr didn't need to know any of that.

The incident that affected me the most happened in Guatemala. I'd taken Bobby Beard's life with my bare hands. It took a long time to move forward from that. It was just so up close and personal, not like using a gun. When Brody and I both shot an assassin, I had no qualms about it at all. It was us or him. Overall though, I'd been shot at more times than I'd ever had a chance to shoot back, mostly thanks to Captain Fred. Now he was involving me in yet another potentially dangerous situation. I wished I could practice with my new weapon, but I only had the one magazine's worth of bullets. Starr had a box of extras, so I'd get him to fire a few rounds so he'd be comfortable with his gun.

"Let's do our system checks," I said. "We leave early tomorrow, so go easy on the booze tonight."

The Caribbean Sea was indeed calm that morning. Even though I didn't care for my destination, it felt good to be going to sea again. I hadn't gotten the chance to become intimate with my new boat yet. I wanted to pay close attention to her sounds and vibrations. I wanted to see what kind of character she had. I knew she came from a good pedigree, but I hadn't put her through the paces yet. She also needed to get to know me a little better if we were going to be good partners.

I carefully eased her out of the slip and crawled slowly out of the marina. Just putting her big engines in gear made her go too fast in the No Wake Zone. I had to keep pulling back to neutral to keep her from throwing big waves at all the cruising boats still tied up. She responded instantly to commands, and the grumbling roar of her engines told me she was ready to run. As soon as we cleared the break wall, I pushed the throttles forward until she got up on plane. I leveled her out at thirty knots and listened to her song. I knew she had plenty more, but I didn't want to push the envelope of our range by burning too much fuel too early in the trip. I set a course slightly north of east and engaged the autopilot. I watched her fuel burn readings for a few minutes. She gulped one hundred gallons per hour without trying.

We were well offshore and certain to make it on fuel when I opened her up. There was a lot more throttle to be had. We were doing forty-five knots in no time. The engines sang at a higher pitch but felt more at ease. She wanted to go all out. Her hull rose up and skimmed across the surface like a much smaller vessel. She was quite fast for her size; surprisingly so. She was also very thirsty at that speed, burning double the fuel. She would only run for six hours at wide-open throttle. Twelve hundred gallons at four bucks per gallon equaled almost five grand flushed out the exhaust for six hours of fun. I pulled back on the throttles and let her settle back down to thirty knots. The temperature gauge never rose one degree. The oil pressure was good. The fuel gauge was the only thing that took a hit.

I patted her high-gloss teak helm and told her she did a good job.

"That a girl, *Miss Six*," I said. "I see what you can do."

She was happy that I'd loosened her reins for a few minutes. She sounded more content now. I committed her song to memory. In the future, any deviation would alert me to trouble. It was a good start. I could sense her communicating with me. She had a soul, unlike some other boats I'd been on. I didn't think I could sell her for something more economical. She was a good girl, and I didn't want to piss off Captain Fred. I'd have to learn to deal with the awful fuel economy.

I slowed to a crawl and told Starr to get his gun. I had some empty beer cans on the bridge that he could plink at. When he was ready, I threw one up and over the side. The shot surprised me. Starr hit the can before it made it to the water. He smiled up at me and pretended to blow smoke from the barrel of his pistol.

"Beginner's luck?" I asked.

"I can hit them at least half the time," he said. "Sitting still I won't miss."

"Good to know, cowboy," I said. "You might make yourself useful yet."

Eventually, we neared the Colombian coast. I slowed down and got my bearings. We turned due north and passed between Isla Manzanillo and Castillogrande as we entered the Bay of Cartagena. The marina was on an island called La Manga. The voices on the radio were all speaking Spanish. When I finally reached Club de Pesca what little Spanish I knew escaped me. I fumbled with what to say and how to say it.

"Atracar para buque cincuenta y quatro," I said. "Berth for a fifty-four-foot vessel."

I didn't understand the answer.

"El bote cincuenta y quatro," I said. "Corbata arriba."

"Si, senor," came the reply. "Numero Quince."

Number fifteen. I needed to find slip number fifteen. I yelled at Starr to look for it.

"It's the last one on this first dock here," he yelled back. "The only empty one on this side."

There was plenty of room to turn around so I could back in, but the slip looked narrow for my seventeen-foot beam. There was a large sailboat on the Tee-head of the pier that I didn't want to get anywhere near. There was a seventy-foot yacht on the other side of me that probably cost ten million dollars.

135

"Grab a boat hook and fend me off if you have to," I yelled to Starr. "It's going to be tight."

I worked the throttles back and forth, using the twin engines to steer in reverse. I was facing the stern with my hands behind me, gently nudging towards the dock. The slip couldn't have been more than eighteen feet wide, leaving me only six inches on either side. Fortunately, there was no wind or current, and I managed just fine. I later learned that the slips were twenty feet wide, so I had eighteen inches extra room on both sides. Still tight, but doable. I wouldn't want to try it with the wind blowing. Starr was quick with the lines, and two dockhands assisted us. I gave them each a ten when we were secure in the slip.

"Your Spanish any better than mine?" I asked Starr.

"I was starting to pick it up some," he said.

"Let's check in with the office," I said. "See how that goes."

I wondered how we were going to navigate the city and deal with our mission in spite of the language barrier. Did this politico speak English? What about cab drivers? In the meantime, there was one very important Spanish word that I knew; cerveza. I was ready for a few cold ones. Starr managed to communicate well enough to pay our slip fee for a week. We put it on Fred's card. The facilities were very nice, maybe even better than Flamenco Marina in Panama. They didn't make you pay extra for amenities either. They did, however, insist that we receive a visit from Customs and Immigration. That would ruin my plan to end my electronic trail in Panama, but we couldn't avoid it. I'd have to leave Colombia without checking out. It would still be confusing enough to anyone looking for me. Of course, I wouldn't check in with the United States Immigration folks either. My passport details would narrow the search for me to Panama or Colombia. I wouldn't be found in either country.

As captain, I was supposed to wait with the boat for an official to arrive, take my money, and fill out the paperwork. I sent Starr off to get some beer and returned to our slip. The guy showed up from the airport in less than thirty minutes. He spoke some English, which was good because there were problems. I hadn't checked out of the last country I'd been traveling in, and I had no courtesy flag for my new country. A crisp hundred dollar bill for the customs agent and a quick trip to the ship's store solved these issues. When Starr boarded with a case of beer I gave one to the agent. He smiled and finished the paperwork without any further delay. The beer was called Poker. It tasted like some of the worst cheap beers I drank in college; Milwaukee's Best maybe.

I walked out past the big sailboat to get a look at the old walled portion of Cartagena. It was a famous port city back in the heyday of piracy. Many goods, but mostly gold, were shipped to Spain in the 1500s. Sir Francis Drake pillaged the city before being convinced to leave with a ten million peso ransom. The local government fortified the city with huge stone structures to prevent future attacks. It became so impenetrable that the English couldn't conquer it in 1741 in spite of bringing 186 ships. Cartagena remained a province of Spain until gaining their independence in 1821.

During the twentieth century it became the focal point for shipping cocaine out of Colombia to points around the world, but especially Miami. Coke garnered less attention now, but it was still being smuggled into Florida on a regular basis. I know because I did it. Legal weed and Mexican heroin were now more prominent, but plenty of black market dope flowed into the States from all over central and South America. Cartagena might appear more modern now, but it retained the aura of its turbulent past.

"Maybe we should buy a bunch of coke while we're here," suggested Starr. "You've got enough money to do it. We could both get rich."

"We could both go to jail or be killed," I responded. "We've got no one to sell it to and no connections. We're just two stupid gringos in a strange land. Dumb idea."

"People do it all the time," he said. "Or at least they used to."

"It all has to be arranged beforehand," I told him. "The purchase and the sale have to be planned out. You don't just stroll into South Beach and unload a kilo of coke on the street."

"I guess not," he said. "Just a passing thought."

"You'll make it to Florida with ten grand in your pocket," I said. "A lot more than what you had when I found you. Be happy with that."

"Point taken," he said.

I didn't know what we were supposed to do next. I didn't have the name of the politician I was supposed to find. I had to call Captain Fred for further instructions.

"We're here, in Cartagena," I said. "Nice marina."

"Your crew still cooperating?"

"Turns out he's a sharpshooter with a revolver," I said. "Hopefully that talent won't be needed."

"Your target's name is Humberto Fajardo," he said. "He lives in the high-end residential district on Manga Island, or Las Manga, La Manga; whatever it's called. Same one you're on now. The streets are all numbers. He's on 24. 110 Calle 24."

"Where's his office?" I asked.

"In the old city," Fred answered. "On a side street off Calle 35. Next to a clothing store called Soloio."

"Where am I more likely to catch him off-guard?"

"At his home," he said. "When in the city, he is always surrounded by people. It's very congested and busy down there. Damn tourists."

"What do I offer him?"

"It's not an offer; it's a demand," he said. "It's up to you to convince him to accept the terms."

"How much?"

"Twenty grand ought to do it," he said.

"Can't you hire some local thugs to do this?" I asked. "You've got to have connections in this country for this kind of work."

"I want him to know that it was my people that got to him," he explained. "Not the Colombian government, not the cartels, but Americans working for me."

"I assume he knows who you are?"

"He knows," Fred said. "He's getting his fifteen minutes of fame by standing in my way."

"How's this guy's English?"

"He got his degree at the University of Florida."

"Is he known to our government?"

"He was on some panel of delegates concerning their border with Venezuela," he said. "Got to shake hands with minority leader McCarthy back in the spring. There's been talk of him switching to one of the majority parties and mounting a bid for president someday, but he's still young."

"How young?"

"Mid-forties," he said. "Sharp looking but starting to go soft in the middle."

"Aren't we all?" I said. "Think he'll resist our persuasion?"

"I think he's expecting it," he said. "Just not this way. If you can invade his privacy, maybe get into his inner sanctum somehow, it will shake him up."

"I'll see what I can do," I said. "I'll need a few days to do the legwork. I'll let you know when it goes down."

"I'm counting on you, son."

I knew then that getting me to Panama wasn't about me taking over the boat. It was about getting me to Cartagena. Starr may not have even lost his job because he was a lousy charter captain. He lost it because Fred was trying to take over half the economy of Colombia. I'd been masterfully manipulated to the point where I couldn't say no. The Hatteras was worth several million easy, but that was money Fred had already spent. All I had to do was convince a politician to accept a twenty grand bribe, and the boat was mine. I didn't have to consider my options for long before I counted out the money.

I grabbed a tourist map from the marina the next morning. Calle 24 was only twelve blocks long, and it began just outside the gates. Starr and I went for a little walk through the neighborhood. There was another marina a few blocks away called Club Nautico. There were thirty or forty boats anchored all around it. We checked it out for curiosity's sake. We found that they allowed dinghy access for the anchored boats. Our marina was a bit more exclusive, which was fine, as long as I wasn't paying for it. Left to my own devices I'd be one of those anchored boats, but I didn't have a dinghy yet. That would be at the top of my list once I settled down in Florida.

The next few blocks featured high-rise hotels on the waterfront. We found Fajardo's house just beyond them. It was a nice place but crammed onto a small lot. He had neighbors just a few feet away on both sides.

"Check for windows in those alleys," I said, dropping my map on the sidewalk.

"Two on the left side," he said. "About four feet off the ground. Some bushes in between."

I got up and walked a little further before I suddenly needed a flip flop adjustment. I stopped again to fuss with my feet.

"One big one on this side," he said. "It's up too high. Doesn't look like it opens."

I recovered, and we walked on. Calle 24 turned away from the water and became Carrera 24, which I didn't understand. Calle meant street. Carrera meant career, at least as far as I could remember. Maybe I had it wrong. We turned left on Calle 25 and walked back towards the marina. The houses behind Fajardo's lined the street to our left. There were no fences between any of the houses. Some had shrubbery, but most did not. There was no room for much of anything between them. There was just enough space for a man to slip away in the dark, undetected.

NINE

We went back the next night well after dark, but not so late that interior lights would be turned off. I wanted to see how much lighting was available and determine the darkest places to approach Fajardo's house. The street outside our marina was well lit, as was the stretch along the high-rises and in front of Club Nautico. From there on it was barely lit at all, except for those houses that had a light fixture in the front yard. No one else was walking in the poorly lit area, though we did notice a few cars passing by.

There was a covered porch at Fajardo's front door, which was lit. There were no other outdoor lights on his property. The neighbor's houses on either side were poorly lit from our point of view. A light shone through the windows on the left side of the house, illuminating the alley. Calle 24 was on the waterfront, but there was a park with a lot of vegetation beside the harbor. The parking area had lights, but the bushes did not.

We kept walking around the corner and started back up Calle 25. It was even darker on this street. Some of the buildings housed a business of one kind or another, and they were all closed for the night. I ducked behind a place called Tienda La Cartujita, which I roughly translated as "Card Store," and checked around back. There was a small courtyard lined with trash cans and cardboard boxes. There was no fence. I couldn't see well enough to know if I could use the common space to make it to the alley alongside Farjado's house. I went back to the street where Starr was acting as a lookout.

"I want to come back with a flashlight," I told him. "I think we can cut through here to get where we need to go, but it's damn dark back there."

"What are we going to do when we get there?"

"Bust in one of those side windows and confront our man," I said. "Slip back this way and disappear."

"If he calls the cops we'll be sitting ducks walking these streets," Starr said. "We need a faster way out of here."

"Let me know when you think of one," I said. "If he accepts the bribe he won't call the cops."

"If he refuses?"

"We'll make it so he's unable to call them, at least right away," I said.

"Not sure I like the sound of that."

"I can do it myself if you want out," I said. "But it would be nice to have another gun handy."

"We're not going to kill this guy, right?"

"Not intentionally," I said.

We kept walking but jumped back over to the lighted area by the high-rises. The neighborhood was surprisingly quiet. All the partying must have been taking place elsewhere. The only real action was the movement of dinghies back and forth from Club Nautico Marina and the anchored boats, which gave me an idea. There were several marine supply stores across the street from our marina. A couple of cheap kayaks would be perfect. Instead of worrying about getting caught on the street, we could escape through the park and quietly paddle away. We wouldn't be out of place amongst the anchored boats, and they would help to conceal us as we made our way back to Club de Pesca and Incognito VI.

Our work was done for the evening. We retired to the Hatteras for a few rounds of rum and beer before calling it a night.

"How did you get so good with a revolver?" I asked Starr.

"My dad was a shooter," he said. "He taught me and let me shoot a lot when I was just a kid."

"He'd probably be reported to child services these days," I said. "But it's cool that you have that skill."

"I always had guns until I went to Panama," he said. "They're pretty free with them for citizens, but not for us gringos."

"I always kept a shotgun handy," I said. "Then I met a former FBI agent, and suddenly we had handguns. Then I moved to the mountains, and we got rifles. I've got a small arsenal in my car back in Fort Myers Beach."

"Shit, I haven't had a car in years."

"I never had one until we moved to the mountains," I said. "My dinghy was my car."

"If you want to live at anchor you're going to need a decent dinghy," he said.

"I was thinking maybe a flats boat or a little skiff," I told him. "Something to run for groceries with, and do a little fishing."

"Plenty of them in Florida," he said. "If we ever get there."

"We'll get there," I said. "As soon as we take care of business here."

The next day we walked over to Aquatica and bought two crappy little sit-in kayaks. We could have found something better at any Walmart back in the States, but we'd only be using them once. There was no way I would take them with me. We put them overboard and practiced paddling around inside the marina basin. They'd do, but just barely. After practice, we headed out into the harbor and paddled through the anchored boats, chatting up any Americans we saw. It was rare for cruisers to get this far south. Most that came down from Mexico stopped at the Rio Dulce in Guatemala. Those that worked their way down through the islands ended up in Grenada or Trinidad. No one wanted much to do with Venezuela anymore.

It was a nice day to be out on the water, so we kept going until we got to the park across the street from our targeted politician's house. We pulled our kayaks up on the bank and sat at a picnic table just watching the activity nearby.

Further down the island were the commercial docks. If you continued around the point, you'd find the industrial area where I'd loaded my old trawler with coke. Around another point were the fuel docks where the local thugs looked for an opportunity to ruin my day. I had no reason to go that far.

There was a huge four-masted schooner tied up between the park and the point. I later learned that *Edurbe* was part of a gathering of tall ships from all over South America. I didn't want to stick around to see the rest of them arrive. I wanted to get this job done and get the hell out of Cartagena. Starr agreed.

"We're just going to bust through a window and hand this dude twenty-grand?" Starr asked.

"I don't anticipate it being unlocked," I answered. "You're welcome to try the front door first."

"What if he has an alarm system?"

"Then we go to plan B," I said.

"What's plan B?"

"I haven't thought of it yet," I admitted.

"Now might be a good time to figure that out."

"If sirens go off and lights come on, we make haste to the kayaks and retreat," I said. "Find another way to get to him."

"Why not walk into his office and have a civilized sit-down with the guy?"

"We are supposed to be instilling fear in him," I said. "It's not a negotiation. It's an ultimatum."

"Take the money, do as you're told, or it will go bad for you," Starr said.

"Much easier to accomplish if he's afraid for his life," I explained. "In his office, he might assume we won't shoot him, especially in broad daylight. When he's lying on his floor in his underwear with a gun to his head, he'll be more inclined to cooperate."

"Assuming there's no alarm."

"Shall we stop by the local ADT office and ask if he's a customer?" I said. "Pop that window and see what happens. Climb through quick before he can get his shit together. Bust him up a little then show him the money. Let him know we'll be watching."

"And merrily paddle away when we're done," he said. "Life is but a dream."

"Sometimes you just have to make shit happen," I said. "You can't always sit around waiting for the perfect opportunity."

"A lesson I should take to heart, I suppose," he said.

We took a slightly different route on the way back to our marina. I led Starr farther away from shore and out beyond the boats in the anchorage. It was longer, but it would make us invisible in the dark. There was no current to speak of, so as long as the wind didn't kick up we'd be fine. I was ready. Starr would assist me, somewhat reluctantly. Breaking and entering in a foreign country didn't appeal to him much. I figured that as long as we were giving money instead of stealing it, we'd be okay. Once an understanding was reached with Fajardo, we could walk out the front door without fearing the police.

I didn't consider the possibility that he would take the money and then attempt to have us arrested. He wouldn't know our names or where we came from, only that we were there on behalf of Fred Ford. The consequences of double-crossing a man as powerful as Fred would be dire. Fajardo would know that.

After dinner, I tried to get some rest, but Starr was too busy to allow it.

"Relax, will you?" I said.

"Aren't you wound up?" he asked. "I can't sit still."

"Worrying won't help a damn thing," I told him. "You're wasting your energy."

"I can't help but worry," he said. "I've never done anything like this before."

"It will be over soon," I said. "In and out fast. Nothing to it. If you're going to pace, do it off the boat. You're bugging me."

He walked up the dock, and I leaned back and closed my eyes. I visualized how it would go down. Once the window was broken, our target would come to us. I'd engage him quickly before he could realize exactly what was happening. Once he was brought down to size, I'd explain his predicament. I'd give him the money and force him to accept. Then we'd casually walk away, leaving him to stew over it. He'd vote in favor of Fred's initiative and spend the money on whores and blow, or whatever he was into.

Starr started bothering me about two in the morning. He saw late-night drinkers on dinghies headed back out to their boats. The bars were closing for the night, and now would be a good time to make our move. I vaguely recalled some military stratagem about three or four in the morning being the optimal time for an attack. Even if our man was late to go to bed, he would certainly be asleep by then. I took the time to make and drink a cup of coffee before preparing for our expedition. Starr seemed wide awake without it.

We checked our weapons and added knives to our arsenal, along with a roll of duct tape. We wore dark clothing and each carried small black flashlights. We paddled out into the harbor just as the last of the dinghies went by on their way to the anchorage. After passing through the fleet, we had a short distance of open water to traverse before we reached the park. No one was on the street or in the parking lot at that hour. We tied the kayaks to some mangroves and let them float instead of pulling them ashore.

Using the bushes, we snuck through the park unseen until we were directly across the street from Fajardo's house. It was completely dark except for the light above the front door. We stayed hidden for a few more minutes, watching the street.

"Slow your breathing," I whispered. "Stay calm and in control. Keep your cool at all times."

"I'm ready," Starr said. "Let's do this thing."

We scurried across the empty street to the alley on the left side of the house. I used my flashlight to check for wires or security devices on the window, but I couldn't be sure. I stuck enough tape on the pane to keep it from shattering too loudly. I looked at Starr. He nodded. We each used the butt of our guns to bash the window. It still made noise, but not that familiar shattering sound. I had to swipe a few remaining shards out of the way. They fell on the carpet and barely made a noise. Starr knelt and cupped his hands to boost me up and in. I grabbed his arms and helped him through. No alarms blared. No lights came on. No occupant appeared. We'd made enough noise to wake most any sleeper, but Fajardo did not come running.

I risked the flashlight to check the layout of the house. There were no bedrooms on the first floor. I pointed at the stairway. It was narrow and steep; a nice place to set up an ambush. Was Fajardo armed and waiting? I grabbed a pillow and threw it up to the landing at the top of the stairs. It landed with a soft thud. Nothing else happened. I shrugged at Starr and began a careful ascent; my pistol held in front of me.

There were two bedrooms on the second floor. One was empty and one housed a deeply sleeping Colombian politician. There was an empty bottle of rum on the nightstand. The man was on his back, with a thin line of drool running from the corner of his mouth. He was wearing silk pajamas. I put the barrel of my gun against his temple. There was no reaction.

"This guy could sleep through an earthquake," I said out loud.

"Is he alive?" Starr asked.

"He's breathing," I said. "Wake up, asshole."

Fajardo stirred and grumbled. I slapped him hard across the face. When he opened his eyes, he saw my weapon pointed at his head. The instilling of fear had been accomplished.

"Good morning, sleeping beauty," I said.

"Who are you?" he asked. "What do you want?"

"We are emissaries of one Frederick Ford," I said. "I believe you've heard of him. We are here to present you with a gift."

"I don't understand."

"A gift with strings attached," I said. "For your vote in favor of the infrastructure initiative."

"It was not necessary to break into my home," he said, trying to sit up.

I used the barrel of the gun to push his head back down onto his pillow.

"It is necessary that you understand how important this is to Mr. Ford," I said. "You will accept this gift, and you will vote in favor."

I increased the pressure to his face and pulled the cash out of my pocket for him to see.

"Do you accept this gift from Mr. Ford?"

"I accept," he said. "Please, don't kill me."

"And you promise on your life that you will vote in his favor?"

"I will," he said. "I will see to the bill's passage."

"Do you understand the consequences if you fail to live up to your word on this?"

"I understand," he said. "I will do as you wish."

"It's not a wish, you worthless piece of shit," I said, jamming my gun hard into his forehead. "It's a command."

"I understand," he said. "I will do as you say."

"Open your mouth," I yelled.

He looked confused by that order, so I put the gun to his lips.

"Open it."

He opened his mouth, and I stuffed the money in it. I thought he might cry. The fear was welling up in his eyes. He'd been easier to break than I'd thought.

"We'll be leaving now," I said. "But we'll be nearby until after the vote. We'll be watching you."

He nodded his understanding. I motioned for Starr to go to the door. I backed out of the room, keeping an eye on Fajardo. He made no effort to get up. Starr led me as I walked backward down the stairs. We went directly to the front door to leave. As we opened it, the alarm sounded. The son of a bitch didn't have his windows wired, but the door set off his security system.

"Go, go, go," I yelled.

We sprinted across the street and into the park. I plopped my ass in the kayak and started paddling like hell. Starr rolled his and fell into the water.

"Get up, damn it," I said. "Last one back is a rotten egg."

I had some experience with a kayak. I concentrated on keeping the bow straight and making long deep pulls with the paddle. I kept my elbows up and angled the paddle straight down as I pulled. Starr's kayak wiggled back and forth as he splashed his paddle, and soon I'd left him behind. I made it out past the boats in the harbor before looking back. Starr was coming along, and no one was following him. I let him catch up before resuming; coaching him on proper technique.

We entered the marina basin side by side just before four in the morning. No one was about, and all was quiet. We tied up the kayaks and slid into the salon without being seen.

"Holy shit I thought my heart was going to beat out of my chest," Starr said, collapsing onto the couch.

"I told you to remain calm at all times."

"I forgot about that when the alarm went off," he said.

"It's over now," I told him. "You can chill out now."

"When can we leave for Florida?"

"As soon as they vote," I said. "As long as our boy votes the way Fred wants him to."

"When is that?"

"I'll ask Fred in the morning."

TEN

Both of us slept well into the afternoon. No cops arrived to disturb us. No Colombian thugs came to give us payback for what we'd done the night before. *Miss Six* floated peacefully in her slip, waiting for her next adventure. I shook off the cobwebs and called Captain Fred.

"He's already called various party leaders to lend his support to the project," Fred said. "Fine job."

"Good to hear," I said. "When is the actual vote?"

"They'll call for it this week," he said. "Now that they know they have enough votes. Right now they're trying to figure out who got him to change his mind, but no one is taking credit for it."

"Fajardo knows," I said. "Trust me on that."

"I knew I could count on you."

"What was holding him up in the first place?" I asked.

"Endangered species habitat," he said. "Damn cartels clear more land for growing coca than any road project ever will. He claims to worry more about frogs and lizards than his constituents."

"I guess the frogs and lizards are worth less than twenty grand."

"It would be hard to find a politician down here that can't be influenced with a little walking around money," he said. "They cost more in the U.S."

"We'll sit tight until after the vote," I said. "But I hope it's soon. I don't have a good vibe about this place."

"Most of the violence is geopolitical," he explained. "The civil war with FARC is over, but new groups have popped up, mainly the ELN. The government is always battling militia groups and the cartels at the same time. Man on the street crime is way down from the past unless you're into drugs. The tourist areas have been relatively safe for the past few years, even Cartagena."

"What about Venezuela?" I asked. "Doesn't that situation bother you, with all the time and money you're investing here?"

"If our government gets involved in Venezuela they'll use Colombia as a base of operations," he said. "There will be government contracts to fill, supplies to move, officers to be kept happy. Wartime is money time, my friend. Did I ever tell you the story about flying the Marcos family out of the Philippines?"

"Several times," I said. "I don't want to be near any war in the third world, but you have at it all you want."

"I suspect the legislature will hand the bill over to the president by Friday," he said. "He'll sign it, but you can split as soon as Fajardo lives up to his end of the bargain."

"Let me know, will you?" I said. "We'll be keeping a low profile until then."

"As soon as I hear the good news," he said. "Thanks, Breeze."

I sat in the cockpit, watching the kayaks bob in the water. I suddenly wanted them gone. I didn't think anyone was looking for us, but they were the only connection to our illicit business with Fajardo. Starr was at the pool, so

I used one kayak to tow the other one out to the anchorage. I went from boat to boat, trying to give them away. Most of the cruisers were well equipped and had no use for them, but I finally found a young couple willing to take them off my hands. All I asked for was a ride back to the marina.

I felt better with them gone. Only Fajardo himself could identify us, and I didn't expect him to come walking down the docks. I kept my gun within arm's reach anyway. Starr had recovered from his fright and was working any angle he could with the few English speakers in the marina. I almost wished he would worm his way onto some other boat, just to be rid of him, but I still felt that I needed him to get back home. The Hatteras was a lot of boat for one person to handle, especially around docks, and I needed to visit several docks for fuel on the way back. It would be good to have his experience with the out of the way stops we needed to make. If I had to make the trip alone, I would, but it would be easier with a little help.

Two days went by with no word from Captain Fred. I was feeling cramped but was wary about leaving the marina grounds and going out into public. The need for groceries was too much to ignore. I wanted to stock up before leaving, but there was no grocery anywhere close. Starr and I took turns trying to communicate with the marina staff; trying to get a ride to a supermarket, or supermercado. We had little success until one of the dockhands pointed at his phone. He pulled up an app called Uber English. Starr took his phone and checked it out. Supposedly it made sure your driver spoke English, no matter where you were in the world. It cautioned that Uber was technically illegal in Colombia, but was quite active, especially in the tourism areas.

Starr made the call, and our driver arrived within ten minutes. He drove a black town car that closely mimicked the legal taxis in Cartagena. His English wasn't great, but it was better than our Spanish. We got our point across, and he took us to a place called The Fresh Market. It was the only store with English labels in the area he explained. He thought we might appreciate that. I did until we saw the prices. It was an upscale gourmet type of grocer, with expensive wine and cheeses. There were just enough actual food choices to fill two bags, but it was all overpriced. I wasn't up to leaving and trying another store, so we made do with what was available. We had the driver stop at La Tienda del Licores on the way back. We grabbed a case of Poker Beer and a bottle of Dictador Rum.

Our semi-English speaking Uber guy asked for ten dollars when we got back to the marina. I gave him a twenty and urged him to keep the change. He didn't argue. His big smile told me he was happy.

"Gracias, amigo," I said.

As we started walking down the docks, we saw two police officers out near the Hatteras. Our arms were full with our booty. The load got heavy after standing frozen for a few seconds.

"Follow my lead," I said to Starr.

I boarded a big cruiser from Canada and set my groceries down. Starr did the same. The cockpit door was unlocked, so I stuck my head inside.

"Anybody home?" I said.

There was no reply, so I waved Starr in with me. I peeked through the curtains but couldn't see the cops.

"What are they doing here?" he asked.

"No idea," I answered. "But there was no point in introducing ourselves."

"I'm with you on that," he said. "How are we going to know when they are gone? What if the owners of this boat show up?"

"All questions and no answers," I said. "I'll go up on the bridge and take a look."

"What if they see you?"

"They don't know this isn't my boat," I said.

He lacked the ability to think on his feet. Unless he was sucking up to some yacht owner, he lacked resourcefulness. It was hard to picture him surviving in Panama for very long. I went back outside and climbed up onto the bridge. The cops had made their way to the end of the dock and were now coming back towards me. I saw some binoculars, so I put them to use, focusing in on the two officers. On their shoulders was a patch that said *Seguridad*. They were security guards, not cops. I don't know why I hadn't seen them before, but they shouldn't be anything to worry about. I waited for them to pass and even waved as they walked by. They waved back and continued walking. I couldn't feel stupid about it. It was better to be safe than sorry.

"The coast is clear," I said. "Just security guards."

"Paranoia got the best of us," Starr said.

"Just staying on our toes," I said. "Always be aware. They could have been cops, and we could have walked right into them."

"Let's go," he said. "Beer's getting warm."

We stepped aboard *Miss Six* and stowed our groceries. I put a few beers in the freezer and sampled a shot of the rum. It had a honey flavor to it, and it went down smooth.

"Dangerous stuff," I said. "Take it easy with this."

He waved off the rum and opened a lukewarm beer. It was bad enough when it was cold. A light was blinking on the SAT phone. I'd missed a call from Fred. I called him back right away.

"The vote is tomorrow," he said. "If our boy cooperates you'll be free to go."

"I predict he will," I said. "If he doesn't?"

"I'll need you to convince him of the error of his ways," Fred said. "He needs to know that breaking a deal with Fred Ford has consequences."

"If he doesn't vote in favor I'll be angry enough to break a few bones," I said. "Just for making me stay here longer, but I hope it doesn't come to that."

"You should embrace the local culture," he said. "Go down to the old city and dance with some pretty girls."

"Is this whole mission just to keep my mind off what happened back in Banner Elk?" I asked. "Sweet boat, expense account, dancing with pretty girls."

"You needed a distraction," he said. "And I needed someone to take care of business in Cartagena. Shit works out."

"A wise man once told me that," I said. "It's been difficult to live by lately."

"It was a tough loss," he said. "I can't take your pain, but you're going to be okay. We'll make a toast to the memory of the lovely Miss Brody when you get back."

"Call me as soon as they take the vote," I said. "I'll get to Florida as quickly as I can."

I decided that I wanted to move the boat out to the anchorage. It would be that much less to do when it was time to go, plus I wanted to familiarize myself with the windlass and how she acted on the hook. If I was going to live at anchor eventually, I might as well get a taste of it now. I plugged the phone back into the charger and told Starr what I wanted to do.

"What if we have to go back after Fajardo?" he asked. "You gave away the kayaks."

"Are you always such a negative thinker?" I asked. "The first questions out of your mouth always come from a negative place. Instead of what can go wrong, why not what can go right? We'll save time and effort by leaving the slip today. It's that much closer to Florida."

"I guess we can always come back in," he said.

"Or find another marina," I said. "There has to be six or seven of them here."

"You're right," he said. "Go settle up with the marina and I'll get her ready to go."

I almost fell for it, but I stopped dead in my tracks. It would be a perfect opportunity for him to leave without me. He had food, fuel, and all my money. I'd be stranded in creepy Cartagena with nothing. He couldn't get away with such thievery in the States, but down here in the Caribbean, there were a million places to hide. I climbed up to the bridge and pocketed the keys. Then I thought he might have a second set hidden away that I didn't know about. I went back inside.

"You're coming with me," I announced.

"You don't need me to pay the tab," he said. "I'll warm her up and loosen the lines."

"No, you won't," I said. "I can't give you the chance to run off while I'm gone."

"After all we've been through?" he said. "You still don't trust me?"

"Money can cause a man to make poor decisions," I said. "And I don't trust anyone, with the possible exception of Captain Fred."

"Fine," he said. "I'll go with you. Happy now?"

"I'll be happy when we make it to Florida."

Fred's credit card paid our bill, and we returned to make the boat ready. I started the engines and had a little chat with *Miss Six*.

"This is just a tease, girl," I told her. "We're not leaving yet. Soon, okay?"

The boats were thick and close together just off Club Nautico. I had to settle for the southern part of the harbor near the commercial docks and cruise ship terminal. It wasn't far from the park across from Farjardo's house. I could swim to it if I had to. It would also make for a quick exit from the area when it was finally time to go.

We feasted on fancy cheese and prosciutto, washing it down with the cheap beer. It didn't fill me up, but I thought that some rum would finish it off nicely. I took two coffee cups out to the cockpit and poured each of us a few fingers of Dictador. We watched the sun go down over Bocagrande.

"I've got to apologize for something," Starr said.

"What's that?"

"I have to admit that it did cross my mind to drive this baby out of here without you," he said. "But I didn't commit to the idea."

"So I wasn't wrong to think you're a no-good bastard."

"I've been winging it by my wits for too long, I guess," he said. "Always looking for the big score."

"Your lack of wits is the problem," I said. "Captain Fred was your gift horse, but you blew it. I'm giving you ten grand to basically be a passenger yet you'd screw me over to get more. Ever hear of Karma? You're going to get a big dose of it someday if you keep it up."

"If you believe in that sort of thing," he said.

"You don't?"

"I don't know, man," he said. "What is that? Buddhism? Hinduism? I'm not a big fan of religions."

"You don't have to be religious to believe that what comes around goes around."

"But does it, really?"

"You mean, can you be an asshole to people your entire life and never have to suffer the consequences?"

"You were quite the asshole to Farjardo the other night," he said. "Doesn't that count?"

I hated to admit that he had a good point. I'd spent a few years trying to atone for my sins, and now here I was right back up to no good. I'd swept in gladly to take his boat and livelihood away from him. I'd terrorized a man on behalf of Captain Fred for my own personal gain. I was racking up some bad karma of my own.

"Now that we're getting all metaphysical," I began. "Let me tell you how it went down for me. I was doing lots of bad shit and going nowhere. I did try to be kind to the people that mattered to me. I attempted to exact justice for anyone that would hurt them, but I was constantly on the wrong side of the law, and in turn on the wrong side of what most people would consider good."

"Then you started thinking about Karma somewhere along the way?" he asked.

"Something like that," I said. "I thought it might be time to even up the scales. I started trying harder to do good. At first, it was for a selfish purpose; to save my soul or whatever, but eventually, I learned that it felt good too. There was a definite reward for helping others instead of hurting them or taking advantage of them. I kept the mythical karmic scales in mind all the time, always trying to make up for my past."

"So how did you end up here?" he asked. "What good did it do?"

"It got my woman killed," I said. "My partner, my reason for living. It got her killed."

"So Karma is bullshit then," he said. "It didn't do you any favors."

"Or maybe I was finally getting my comeuppance," I said. "Karma caught up to me."

"That's a heavy burden to bear," he said. "That's why I don't think about this stuff too much. It will hurt your brain."

"On the other hand, this fine vessel could be considered a reward," I said. "A peace offering from the Gods. Just when I lost it all, I've been given another chance."

"How many chances does a man get?"

"I'm losing count," I said. "I've been up and down a half-dozen times. You'd think I would have learned how to stay up by now."

"Maybe there's no meaning to any of it," he said. "We're born. We do the best we can with the circumstances we're given. We die."

"I've always thought there had to be something more," I said. "But we're not meant to understand it while we're here. Mankind has been trying to figure it all out for thousands of years. We still don't know who's flying this rock."

"Right now you're not helping anyone but yourself," he said.

"I'm helping Fred," I said. "I'm helping you whether you realize it or not."

"You took my job and my boat," he said.

"You lost your job and your boat through your own actions," I said. "I could have left your ass to rot in the jungle."

"Fair enough," he said. "But you won't sell me on your Karma nonsense. The meaning of life is that there is no meaning. If I see a shot at something better, I'm taking it. Looking out for number one."

"I wasn't selling anything," I said. "Do what you want. Just don't take a shot at me."

I capped the rum and went inside. Something about Starr didn't sit right with me. He seemed harmless enough, but I couldn't be sure he wouldn't turn on me given the right opportunity. If Fajardo voted yes, we'd begin our journey across an ocean together. I'd have to sleep with one eye open the entire trip. I put my gun under my pillow and considered dumping him before he could dump me.

The sound of small waves lapping the hull took me back to my previous life on a boat. I loved that old trawler, but *Leap of Faith* was a junker compared to *Miss Six*. I couldn't believe it was mine. I'd been too busy to appreciate just how nice she was. I pictured us together in Pelican Bay, watching the dolphins hunt for fish. I said a silent prayer to an unknown God for Farjado to do the right thing.

ELEVEN

Colombia's equivalence to our House of Representatives met in full session the next day to vote on a massive infrastructure bill mostly financed by American businessman and financier Frederick Ford. There was little debate as the wheels of government had turned mostly behind the scenes. There was plenty of pork to go around for various lawmakers to tout during future campaigns. Those previously opposed or on the fence had been sufficiently goaded or bribed to vote in favor. The bill squeaked through when the gentleman representing Cartagena signaled his approval.

"Your work there is done," Fred said. "All's well that ends well."

"Great news," I said. "We'll be leaving immediately. I'm going to turn this phone off but I'll check in as soon as we reach Florida."

"I owe you for this one," he said. "Dinner is on me when you get here."

"You don't owe me a thing," I responded. "This boat is beyond payment. If anything, I still owe you plenty."

"Enjoy it for me," he said. "Just be careful out there."

I put the phone away and yelled for Starr to prepare to raise anchor. I tucked my pistol in my waistband and went to the bridge to start the engines. As soon as they warmed up, we left Cartagena in our wake. Ten hours later, we were back at Shelter Bay Marina in Panama. The ominous feeling that plagued me in Colombia lifted. I even paid for Starr's dinner at the restaurant.

"I was playing around with the chartplotter today," I said. "I couldn't find a marina that was convenient for us within our range."

"Not stopping at a marina," he said. "But we'll get fuel at Bluefields in Nicaragua."

"What's there?"

"Nice big protected bay," he said. "There's a ferry that runs out to an island called El Bluff. It gets fueled at Terminal Atlantico. We can't stay overnight, but we can get good diesel."

"How far?"

"A little over three hundred miles," he said. "Three-twenty or thereabouts."

"Another day, another thousand gallons," I said.

"Not my problem anymore," he said. "But I told you so."

"She's a fuel hog, that's for sure," I said. "Where to after that?"

"That's the messed up part," he said. "There's nothing on the coast of Honduras but jungle. We need to make it five hundred miles to those offshore islands I was telling you about. We have our choice of marinas once we get there. There's a real nice one in Calabash Bight, but Jonesville Point is closer to the mainland, and our next stop."

"Belize?"

"It's an easy run to San Pedro," he said. "Hundred and fifty miles. Good place to hang out a few days."

"Can we make it from there to Grand Cayman?"

"Easier to go up to Quintana Roo," he said. "Easy jump from there to Cuba."

"Do we have to check-in and stamp our passport at all these places?"

"Customs is easily bribed," he said. "Cuba doesn't care as long as you have American dollars to spend."

"That five hundred mile leg is going to be a pain in the ass," I said. "That's well beyond our range at cruising speed."

"I ran it at ten knots," he said. "Stayed far enough offshore that I wouldn't hit anything and napped with the autopilot on."

"How did you get weather information?"

"Didn't," he said. "Kept my nose to the wind and an eye on the sky."

"Any place we can duck into if it gets snotty?"

"Some coves here and there," he said. "Skinny water, mangroves, skeeters the size of cats."

"Any reason why you erased your track on the plotter coming down here?"

"I never thought I'd be going back," he said. "I had it in mind to remain an ex-pat."

"I can leave you off here if you like," I said. "You've got five grand to make a start with."

"I'd rather have ten grand and make my start in Florida," he said. "The jungles of Panama ain't all they're cracked up to be."

"I'm right there with you," I said. "Good old U. S. of A."

We left early the next day to make the run to Bluefields. I'd never been to Nicaragua. There had never been a reason to visit. I could add it to my bingo card of foreign countries once we got fuel. The total fuel bill for the trip would be astronomical, but I doubt Fred would blink an eye when he got his credit card bill. I was out twenty grand for the bribe to Farjado. The fuel cost would come close to equaling that.

There was a light chop on the ocean that did nothing to disturb the Hatteras. We maintained thirty knots of speed the whole way, slowing when we neared the island of El Bluff. We followed the ferry channel to a big concrete dock. I hovered while Starr deployed fenders. Someone was yelling over the radio in Spanish that I couldn't understand. A man came running out to greet us.

"Diesel," I said. "Por favor."

The man pointed and gestured. Starr and I fumbled with our Spanish. Eventually, we figured out that we weren't close enough for the fuel hose to reach us. The three of us used lines to walk the boat closer to shore, eventually hitting bottom. The ferry boat was a shallow draft pontoon, and the facility wasn't designed for visiting vessels. The man shrugged and went to pull out his hose. It was long enough to reach the starboard side tank, but a few feet short of making it to the port side tank.

We had over five hundred miles to go before making another fuel stop. We couldn't afford to try it without completely full tanks. I dug deep into my rudimentary knowledge of Spanish for the correct word for tide.

"Marea?" I asked.

The man motioned with his hands that it was falling.

"Cue cae," he said. "Abajo."

I didn't know either of those words, but I understood that the tide was going out. We needed to pull the boat out to deeper water soon, or we'd be stuck until it came back in. A light bulb went off in the fuel attendant's head, and he went running back up the dock. Starr and I had no idea what that meant either. He came running back with a section of hose that the fuel nozzle would fit into. He spoke at us in rapid-fire Spanish and made some more gestures.

He wanted us to stick this extra hose into the tank fill, and then he could put the nozzle in the other end. It was just long enough for everything to reach. We worked quickly, keeping an eye on the water level in the bay. I paid in cash for the fuel, tipping the man generously. When we went to leave the dock, it was clear we were dead on the bottom. The last thing I wanted to do was spend the night on a concrete dock in Nicaragua. I put both engines in reverse and throttled up hard, churning mud and sending spray all over the back of the boat and the dock. Slowly we inched back until the hull freed itself from the bottom. I got off the throttles and let the wind push us away from the concrete before easing out of there.

We slogged along at a tediously slow speed for two hundred miles until we reached the border of Honduras. The entire coast had been a deep green jungle and remained primitive looking, as we rounded a cape at Iralaya. We had been protected from the northwest wind until then, but now the seas were churning. There was heavy rain inland causing dark water to pour into the sea along the coast. The skies ahead were ugly and menacing. I searched the GPS for shelter from the storm. There was a small inlet ahead leading into a body of water listed as Laguna de Caratasca. The chart did not designate depths in the inlet or the lake. I called for Starr to come take a look.

"Do you know anything about this place?" I said, pointing at the chart plotter.

"No, but we're getting beat up out here," he said. "Can't be good for our fuel mileage either."

"I'm going to nose up close," I said. "When the time comes I want you on the bow. Read the water and yell loud."

The immediate shoreline was rocky, but it turned to sand before we reached the lake entrance. We were in thirty feet of water very close to the beach. Our bow was pointed directly into the oncoming waves, which slowed our speed by several knots. The fuel burn was too high, and the ride was uncomfortable. We were also both tired. We needed to get out of the waves and hole up for a rest and to wait for better weather.

I turned to the southeast to attempt to line up with the inlet and the boat started rocking precariously from side to side. She was built for offshore use, but I wasn't driving her properly for the conditions. I needed to give her some more throttle to get the bow up and stay on top of the waves, but I couldn't risk using up the fuel. It was too dangerous for Starr to be up on the bow. I yelled, but I didn't think he heard me. I saw him start to inch his way forward. He had a lifejacket on. I yelled again through the windshield.

"Forget it," I screamed. "It's too rough. Go back."

I scanned the surface, but all I could see was breaking waves. I looked for a slot of clean water that would indicate enough depth for us to pass, but I didn't see any such thing. The depth finder now told me we had only five feet at the bottom of a trough. We rose up on a wave, and it read twelve feet. I slowed even more and looked again as we rose up another time. There was nothing but breakers. The inlet was impassable. Before we could bottom out, I swung us around and bashed my way back offshore into deeper water.

Starr joined me on the bridge. He was soaked with saltwater and looking none too happy.

"This is some shit, man," he said. "We're going to get clobbered out here."

"Study that chart," I instructed. "Find us someplace to get inside."

"There is nothing," he said. "At least until we round this point at Puerto Castilla. By then we'll almost be to the next fuel stop."

He played with the machine for a minute.

"Looks like good water going in here at Jericho," he said. "But that's only thirty-five miles from the island we want to reach."

"How far from here?"

"One seventy-five," he said.

"Son of a bitch," I said. "That's a long way to limp along like this."

"I don't see any other option," he said. "We might not make it on fuel as it is."

The wave height increased further offshore, but the distance between them was greater. In order to keep the fuel consumption low enough, I had to slow down to eight knots, which was basically idle speed. Up and down we went, sometimes barely making any headway. The engines droned on, hour after hour. They didn't like low rpm's. They wanted to get up and go. I didn't blame them. If only they weren't so thirsty.

Starr took his turn at the wheel, but there was no sleeping down below. The engine noise and the vibrations combined with the action of the waves to render sleep impossible. I made a quarter of a pot of coffee. Any more and it would have spilled out all over the place. It was enough for two cups. I carefully carried one to Starr and then went back to get a cup for me. I was learning that conditions could be just as miserable on a three million dollar boat as they were on my old fifty thousand dollar trawler.

I went back to the bridge as soon as I finished my coffee. We couldn't see the waves coming in the dark. Every once in a while, an odd one would hit us funny and pitch the boat around like a toy. I didn't like the looks of the fuel gauges. I messed around with the chartplotter for a while but could find no escape. We had no choice but to keep pounding along. The weather got worse as we went. It was now raining so hard we couldn't see the bow. Starr stared at the electronics, trying to hold us in a straight line. If there was anything out there to run into, we wouldn't know it until it was too late, even at our slow speed.

"It's a motherfucking monsoon," Starr said. "I hope there are no reefs out here. This is nuts."

"The chart shows nothing but blue water," I said. "Deep blue malevolence at the moment."

"The sea can be a real bitch sometimes," he said.

"If patience is worth anything, it must endure to the end of time," I said.

"What?"

"And a living faith will last in the midst of the blackest storm," I finished.

"Quoting scripture now?" he asked.

"Mahatma Gandhi," I said. "Squirrely little fellow, but he had big faith."

"I have faith that we're good and screwed," he said. "I don't think we're going to make it on fuel."

He was probably right. It was going to be damn close, but we couldn't afford to be dead in the water under these conditions. We'd end up as flotsam on a Honduran Beach. Still, we pushed on; making terrible time and burning up more fuel. The goal was the island of Roatan, which by all my calculations was slightly beyond our range. At Puerto Castilla, we would have to decide. We couldn't anchor in the open sea with these waves. We needed shelter from the wind to do that. If we attempted to cross from the mainland to the island and ran out of fuel, it could prove disastrous.

The engines made our decision for us. I'd been listening closely the entire trip. The pitch changed ever so slightly before the first hiccup occurred. We'd be out of fuel very soon. I skirted close to shore as we rounded the point and headed towards the inlet at Jericho. The wind and seas were now on our stern, pushing us along, so I cut back on the throttles. I had to run very close to the beach before turning south and entering calmer water. The first thing we saw was a bridge that was too low for us to go under. There were several boats tied up at a dock just at the base of the bridge. Before I could get close enough to find a place for us to tie up, the engines quit one after the other. I turned the wheel hard to starboard and used our momentum to drift further into the lee of land. We were completely out of the wind, but drifting towards the bridge. I yelled for Starr to ready the anchor. He ran up and freed it, and I used the windlass to drop it quickly before we plowed into the boats at the dock. The chain came tight, and we spun around to face the current. The anchor stuck and held us fast. I slowly let out more chain until I was satisfied that we would hold steady. The current pulling us back would help the anchor to dig deep and stay put.

"Welcome to Bumfuck, Honduras," I said to Starr. "Where we will remain until we can figure out how to get some diesel."

"Those boats at the dock have to be getting fuel from someplace," he said.

"I suspect they're all gasoline," I replied. "But we can find out after I've slept for twenty hours straight."

"How are we going to get over there?"

"If we can't flag somebody down we'll have to swim," I said. "Looks deserted at the moment. Let's get some rest."

I took some rum back up to the bridge to study the GPS. It didn't show features on land like Google Maps, but you could make out roads and towns. There was something to our south a few miles. I looked over at the docks by the bridge a few times. There was no sign of movement. The weather was too shitty for anyone to think of using a boat. They looked like fishing vessels; worked hard and weathered. We were only thirty or forty yards off the shore, but at least a hundred yards from the docks. I wondered what type of nasty critters swam these waters. Did Honduras have gators or piranhas? I drank a big slug of rum to help me sleep and went to bed. It was all going to have to wait until I got some rest.

Sleep came quickly, and the images of Brody came soon after. It wasn't a typical dream, but rather a slideshow of images depicting all the good times we shared. In each image, she was more beautiful than the last. It ended with a close-up of her face; eyes twinkling like stars in the sky. She smiled and then she was gone.

I woke up a thousand miles from nowhere with no fuel. It was still raining hard, and the wind shook the treetops onshore. No one stirred around the docked boats. I went to start the generator before remembering that we had no diesel. I couldn't even make coffee. Starr came out of his bunk looking like hell.

"A fine mess," he said. "A miserable day in a miserable place."

"We'll get out of here," I said. "Have some patience."

"And some faith?" he asked. "I'm a little short right now."

I got the SAT phone, turned it on, and called Captain Fred.

"Where are you?" he answered. "There's a tropical system developing off the Yucatan."

"Someplace called Jericho in Honduras," I told him. "Out of fuel and desperate. Where's the storm going?"

"Into the Gulf," he said. "Might be a hurricane by the time it gets to Florida. Stay where you are until it's gone."

"There is nothing here," I said. "I need to figure out a way to get some diesel to the boat, at anchor."

"Jericho, Honduras," he said. "Hold on, let me bring you up on maps."

There was a pause, but I could hear computer keys clicking in the background.

"You say you're anchored up," he said. "Are you near a bridge?"

"Yes," I said. South side of the inlet, out of the wind and close to shore."

"About two miles south is a town," he said. "Trujillo. It has an airport and hotels. Gateway to Roatan."

"Take the road at the bridge and go south?"

"Looks like it would be easier to follow the beach," he said. "There's hotels and bars and such all around the airport. Can't miss it. Has to be fuel there."

"That's what I needed," I said. "Thanks."

"How the hell did you run out of fuel?"

"Long story," I said. "Let's just say this boat has very limited range."

"You're resourceful," he said. "You'll figure it out."

"Any timeline on this tropical system?"

"It's supposed to head north of Cuba and towards the Keys," he said. "Maybe even go under the Keys and over to the Atlantic side. The Gulf will be a mess for four or five more days at least. What's your next stop?"

"Roatan, then Quintana Roo," I said.

"Sit tight on Roatan," he said. "Enjoy life for a few days."

"Sounds good," I said. "As soon as we get some fuel."

"Small boats on big oceans," he said. "Does it feel good to be back?"

"Living the dream," I said. "Living the dream."

I went out to survey our situation. The nearest shoreline was covered in thick mangroves. I could see sand further out towards the opening of the inlet. I could swim that far, but I couldn't swim back with a couple of cans of diesel. Too bad I didn't keep those cheap kayaks. Starr said he was a good swimmer, but the sandy beach was a bit of a reach for him. I told him the water had to be shallow enough to stand close to shore. We could swim in at the shortest point, then walk in the water until we made it to the sand.

"How do we get the fuel out to the boat?" he asked.

"Good question," I replied. "I'll let you know when I have an answer."

We had no choice but to travel light. I stuffed a wad of cash in a zippered pocket in my swim trunks and kicked off my flip flops. We'd be walking on the beach for the most part. We stood on the transom for a minute, loosening our arms and stretching; putting off the inevitable.

"You ready?" I asked Starr.

"No, but let's get it over with."

We dove in and started swimming with the current, which threatened to pull us out to sea. We managed to swim across it and get close enough to shore to stand and walk. The bottom was pure muck, which made for slow going, but we managed to trudge past the mangroves and reach the sand. We encountered no gators or piranhas on the way, but there was no way we could swim against the current to get back to the boat.

We walked out around the point and came almost immediately to a cabin with a pool. It looked like a vacation rental or a wealthy person's retreat. We went up and knocked and were greeted by the cleaning lady. She spoke no English and communication was futile. We walked on until we came to a pier with a restaurant. It was a good old fashioned pizza joint called Pizzeria Restaurante El Muello. If the weather were nicer, the view would have been amazing. The pizza was lousy. We were told there was a Texaco in Trujillo, near the airport. We walked on past more cabins and cabanas that all looked private. Finally, we came to a row of bars and hotels that serviced the airport. There were taxis lined up in front of the single terminal.

"Diesel? Texaco?" I asked the drivers.

We walked a few more blocks until we found the gas station. They sold five-gallon gas cans, but only had four of them. I bought the cans and filled them with diesel, but twenty gallons wouldn't get us to Roatan.

"Now what?" Starr asked.

"Take these back to the airport and get a ride," I said.

He shrugged, and we started walking. The cans got heavy almost immediately. The pavement wasn't kind to our bare feet. We were both worn out by the time we got back to the row of taxis. I tried again, asking for a ride to Jericho. No one wanted to carry two ragged gringos with four gas cans, but money talks, even in Honduras. We put our cans in the trunk of a yellow "Teletaxi" and got in the back seat.

"Jericho?" the driver asked.

"Puente," I said. "Bridge."

When we neared the bridge, he gave us a quizzical look. I pointed to the dirt road leading to the docks.

"Aqui," I said. "Here, stop. How do you say, stop?"

"Detener," Starr said. "Detener aqui."

"Espere?" I asked. "Can you wait?"

"Cuanto tiempo?" he asked.

"Five minutes," I said. "Cinco minutos."

We quickly lugged the gas cans down to the dock and returned to the cab. No one was around. We went back to the airport in search of more cans. After much confusion and frustration, we found an auto parts store and a mechanics shop. The parts place only had two gas cans. The mechanic across the street led us out back to somewhat of a junkyard. When he opened the door to a rundown shack, I thought it would fall off. Inside he pointed at a couple of rusty metal cans from the pre-plastic era.

"Cinco dolares para uno," he said.

I looked at Starr.

"Five dollars each," he said.

I handed the man ten bucks, and we carried our collection back to the Texaco. I put a quart of diesel in each metal can and swished it around before dumping it out. It came out brown with rusty flakes. I'd made enough mess already, so I didn't rinse them any further. We now had forty gallons of diesel. Was it enough? I'd figure it out once we got it back to the boat. First, we had to walk to the airport and convince another taxi driver to take us to the bridge.

They all refused. We sat on a bench in front of the terminal with sore feet. The rain started up again. I'm sure we were a sorry sight, which may have caused a cab driver to feel sorry for us. He motioned for us to get in, already knowing where we wanted to go. He dropped us off, and we carried our cans down to the dock and added them to our collection. There was no point in asking him to wait. We'd exhausted the supply of fuel containers in Trujillo.

"Here we are," said Starr. "And there's our boat out there."

"And there are several boats right here in front of us," I said. "Pick one."

"You want to steal one of these boats?"

"Borrow is more appropriate," I said. "One of us is still going to have to swim after we return it."

"That would be you," he said. "The current just about killed me the first time."

"Look for one with the keys in it," I instructed.

We looked over the available inventory. All of them were rough, but at least some of them had to run. We didn't find any keys, but we found such simple systems that they'd be easy to hotwire. We loaded our eight cans of diesel on a small workboat, and I got up under the dash to pull some ignition wires. I used a rusty filet knife to cut the red and white ones, twisted them together, and listened to the engine crank. It didn't start. Starr advanced the throttle, and I tried again. It cranked over, spitting and sputtering, and fired up. A big cloud of smoke rose over the dock, and the noise was deafening. I left the throttle advanced so she could warm up while Starr got the lines. As soon as I put it in gear it died. The current held us against the dock. I quickly jumped the ignition again and threw it into gear the second it fired up.

I almost smashed into another boat but yanked the wheel hard over to avoid the collision. Starr fell on his ass behind me.

"You jump on board and I'll throw you a line," I yelled. "She's not going to keep running at idle."

"Can you at least slow down a little bit?" he asked. "Jesus Christ, risking my life in Bumfuck Honduras with this crazy fucker."

"We gotta do what we gotta do," I said. "Or be stuck here forever."

I ran her up hard alongside the Hatteras, pulling back on the throttle at the last second. As expected, she died, but we got close enough for Starr to jump across. I had a line over to him in an instant. He hung on tight and got control, pulling the old workboat alongside *Miss Six.* I handed over the cans one by one.

"Start dumping them in while I take this back," I said. I'll swim out to you in a bit."

"How are you going to buck that current?"

"I'll walk through the mangroves until it's working with me," I said. "I'll be alright."

"Snakes and God knows what else," he said. "Better you than me."

The old, borrowed boat started easier this time. Starr cut me loose, and I swung her around and steered her back to her berth. I left a twenty under a rusty wrench on the dash for her owner. I walked back out the access road, skirted the outer edge of the mangroves, and found my way back down to the water's edge. I didn't encounter a single snake, but I was again exhausted. I swam out to a sandbar and stood to rest before jumping in again and making the final leg to the boat. Starr sat by eight empty fuel cans.

"Think it's enough?" he asked.

"Give me a minute," I said. "I've had enough for one day."

TWELVE

It was not going to be enough. When we rounded Puerto Castilla, we were thirty-five miles from Roatan, but we traveled another ten miles to get to safety at Jericho. The trip across was now at forty-five miles. The boat burned ten gallons per hour at idle speed. We needed to fill all eight fuel cans again to have a chance to make it.

Obtaining forty gallons of fuel and getting it back to the boat was an all-day affair. The swimming portion of the event had been treacherous. The walking had been tiresome. Stealing a boat had completed our triathlon. The thought of doing it all over again was disheartening, but otherwise, we'd be stuck. We were low on food and water as well. I missed the economy of my old trawler. *Leap of Faith* may have been slow, but she had triple the range of *Miss Six*. The only times I'd ever had to worry about fuel was on boats other than *Miss Leap.*

The situation sucked, there was no doubt about that, but it had to be dealt with. I couldn't blame Starr. If the weather had been nice, we would have cruised into our intended destination without worry. Fred had said the storm was moving into the Gulf, which was away from us. Our local weather would be improving, so we had that going for us. There was nothing more to do that day. My energy reserves were used up, and I was hungry. We had some canned goods, but no way to heat them up. I didn't dare use a drop of fuel running the generator. We still had to bleed the fuel lines to get things running again. On *Miss Leap,* that meant one system. On *Miss Six* it meant two engines and a generator. The Hatteras was a huge step up from the old trawler, but it also meant more systems and more things to fix.

We ate the last of the fancy cheese and washed it down with beer. Starr found a can of peanuts that I didn't know we had.

"We should eat a decent meal when we get back to that town," he said.

"Can't argue with that," I said. "Is there a good restaurant at this marina we're trying to get to?"

"More of a bar and grill," he said. "But they serve fresh fish and cold drinks."

"Great. Is there a place to get groceries?"

"Got to be something around there," he said. "Won't be cheap, I can tell you that. Great island but nothing is cheap."

"We've got to get there first," I said.

"I know we can get supplies in Belize," he said. "Quintana Roo, too. Not a problem."

"Then it's only two more legs to Key West," I said. "You sure we can't jump from San Pedro to Cuba?"

"It's a little more than three hundred and fifty miles," he said. "We can make it, but it's pushing it a little, at least at running speed. Do you want to risk it or play it safe?"

"Right now I vote for playing it safe," I said. "But I've had enough of Latin America. It was my intention to be in Florida. I only got to spend a few days there before starting this escapade."

I tried to do the math in my head. If we ran at thirty knots, burning one hundred gallons per hour, our maximum range was three hundred and sixty miles. Depending on sea conditions, we might be able to run a little slower and stay on plane, which would allow us to make it on fuel. Any tiny disturbance in a perfect plan would ruin it. Conditions had to be perfect. I couldn't count on that to happen. It was always good to have a little wiggle room. I gave up thinking about it and went to bed.

We were greeted in the morning by the sounds of an angry Honduran. Both of us went out to investigate. There was a man on the boat we had borrowed, and he was not a happy camper. I guess the twenty bucks I left onboard didn't appease him.

"What's he saying?" I asked Starr.

"All I caught was chingada," he replied. "It's kind of a universal curse. Might mean fuck, shit, or son of a bitch."

"He must have a car," I said. "He didn't walk here."

"He seems a bit mad to ask for a ride."

"I bet he knows what a hundred dollar bill is," I said. "Let's get his attention."

We started yelling and waving at the old guy, who looked at us with disdain. *What could two crazy gringos on a yacht want with me?* He shook his head and went into his cabin. A few minutes later we heard the creaky old engine fire up. Smoke rolled from the stack as he revved her up good. Soon he was headed our way. I instructed Starr to help me deploy some fenders and waved for the old man to come alongside. He tossed us a line, and we secured him. He gave us a look that likely meant, *now what?*

I dug deep to recall my high school Spanish.

"Necesitamos diesel," I said, pointing to our motley collection of cans. "How do you say pay?"

"Paga," said Starr. "Show him a hundred."

"Cien dolares," I said. "Trujillo para diesel."

"Doscientos," he said. "Hijos de puta."

"He wants two hundred," Starr translated. "Because we're cocksuckers."

"Estupido," the old man said. "Te llevo por doscientos."

"He says we're stupid, but he'll take us for two hundred," Starr said.

"I figured that much," I said. "Start handing cans over before he changes his mind."

I gave the guy two hundred bucks, and we headed to the docks with our cans. He had an ancient pickup truck that was more rust than not. He made us ride in the back with the cans. We jumped out at the Texaco to fill them, but the old man stayed in his cab. It was clear that we were disturbing his day. I would have tried to smooth things over if not for the language barrier. Maybe the money would make up for the fishing days he'd lost due to the weather. The ride back was no more pleasant, but I could taste our escape.

After the fuel cans were loaded back onto the Hatteras, I asked the man to wait.

"Espere," I said. "Por favor."

I grabbed an electrical repair kit from inside and showed it to the old fisherman. He nodded, which I took for permission. I snipped the ignition wires and skinned the ends clean before rejoining them with butt connectors. I reached up from under the dash and turned the key. The engine turned over. The boat was as good as we'd found it.

"Vamonos," he said.

I think he meant for us to beat it, so I got back onboard the Hatteras. Starr tossed his lines, and he puttered back to the docks. He probably had no need to fish now that we'd paid him. I pictured his rusted truck parked outside his local beer joint for the rest of the day.

We dumped forty more gallons of diesel in the tanks and started the tedious task of bleeding the fuel lines. I was new to these engines and this particular set-up. Starr hadn't had to perform this duty on this boat, but he was a wizard with wrenches. He knew exactly what to do and made short work of the job.

"You should be a boat mechanic," I said. "I understand it pays well."

"Only if you work for yourself," he said. "I don't have the discipline to run my own business."

"It could be an honest living for you."

"Honest?" he asked. "Was that money we got down in Panama from an honest living?"

"Depends on how you look at it," I said. "But I see your point. I'm still holding onto some cash that didn't quite come honestly."

"Yet you expect me to get a real job and actually work for a living," he said, practically spitting it out.

"I seem to have been more successful at dishonest work than you," I pointed out. "And better at keeping Captain Fred happy. If you can't cut it on the outskirts of society, maybe you ought to think about rejoining it."

"I'd rather blow my brains out," he said. "Or starve to death in a Honduran jungle."

"I don't want to see you do either," I said. "But you have a gun, and the jungle is a short swim away."

"I'll take my chances back in Florida," he said. "I agreed to help you get there. I'll keep my end of the bargain."

"The wind has been decreasing," I said. "By tomorrow we should be fine to jump across. Things will look better once we have full fuel tanks and full bellies."

"Bust out the crackers and potted meat," he said. "Tonight, we celebrate."

After a few beers, I felt bad about pushing Starr's buttons. There had been a time when I was in worse shape than he was. My only saving grace back then was that I owned a boat. Without it, I would have been homeless, broke, and without hope. I used her to haul weed; first to Punta Gorda and later to the Keys. Eventually, her hold was filled with cocaine for one big score. I made a fragile truce with the

Keys biggest drug kingpin and escaped that life with enough money to survive for quite a while.

After that, I ran missions for Captain Fred and was paid handsomely. Those jobs involved boats and bullets. I realized that flirting with danger on a regular basis wouldn't end well, so Brody and I fled to the mountains. Danger found us there too. Now Brody was gone. No one had shot at me on this trip, but I still felt that familiar tingle up my spine. I wasn't sure if it was Starr or something that lay in wait for us between here and Florida, but my gut was telling me to be aware.

I thought about the remaining legs of our trip. I knew from previous trips in the region that the currents ran northwest from here to the Yucatan Peninsula, then north into the Gulf. We'd have them on our stern for most of the way. Around Cuba, the current ran east below the Keys, then curled around to the north along the east coast of Florida. Current flow along the west coast of Florida was generally to the north and not as strong. If we stuck to Starr's suggested route, none of the remaining legs were too far for our fuel range. It should be all downhill from here.

Once I got settled into life in Florida, I could deal with the fuel issue. I could anchor up in Pelican Bay and only use diesel to run the generator when I needed. I could make short runs to Punta Gorda or Fort Myers Beach for supplies. I could even return to my old marina near Cape Haze from time to time. They provided waste pump-outs and freshwater. The Publix was a long walk, but I could probably get a ride. The occasional longer trip wasn't out of the question but would have to be limited if I wanted my money to last.

I was looking forward to being alone. I still hadn't properly processed the loss of Brody and Red. I needed some time for quiet contemplation if I wanted to work through that. My need for revenge had gone on the back burner. I needed to think about that too. If I wanted to mount a serious campaign to go after her killer, my head needed to be on straight. I'd have nothing but time once this affair was over.

Starr had his head in a cabinet of canned goods. I still didn't want to run the generator until we had full fuel tanks. He produced a can of tuna to round out our gourmet meal.

"So, tell me about Roatan," I said.

"All the tourist action is down at Coxen Hole," he said. "But no facilities for a boat this size. Not much to do in Jonesville, but we need fuel most of all. We'll be more in monkey and sloth territory than the zipline and dive shop area. We could anchor down there if you want after we fill up."

"Probably not my speed," I said. "Let's just get our diesel and move on."

"You want to spend a few days in San Pedro?"

"Where's the fuel dock there?" I asked.

"Downtown San Pedro," he said. "It's where all the dive boats and parasailers fuel up. Good safe diesel."

"How far from Caye Caulker?"

"Ten, twelve miles," he said. "You know they have a resort there now."

"Can't stop progress," I said. "Forget it. I'd prefer to get to Florida as fast as possible. Let's top off the tanks and haul ass up to Quintana Roo in one day."

"We could almost make it straight to Key West from Cancun," he said. "If you really want to skip Cuba."

"Almost?" I asked. "How almost are we talking about?"

"It's about four hundred miles."

"That's a big nope," I said. "We'll keep fuel in this baby and run her at speed without worrying."

"Fine by me," he said.

We stayed awake long enough to kill our beer supply. The breeze had died down completely, and the mosquitoes came out in force. It would be good to leave this place. The lack of wind was a good omen. There was still a chance we could run out of fuel before we made Roatan.

We were both up early and raring to go the next morning. Coffee would have been nice, but we went without it. Starr had the engines purring just as the sun rose over Laguna Guaimoreto to our east. We used the early light to feel our way out of the inlet and back out to sea. I was gentle on the throttle even though there were no waves. It was a total slicker, as some fishermen say. We coasted at a painfully slow seven knots on our way northward. The wind stayed down, the engines kept running, and we pulled into Jonesville Point Marina in the middle of the afternoon.

We went straight to the fuel dock and took on almost twelve hundred gallons of diesel at four

213

dollars per gallon. Our slip was a small finger pier in front of the bar. *Miss Six* dominated the landscape and the view of the few diners in attendance. As soon as we got tied up, we retired to that bar. Salva Vida was the beer of choice in Honduras. It tasted fine and went down easily. We ordered up the catch of the day and told the English speaking bartender to keep the beers coming.

The dinner entrée was whole snapper over rice. I normally preferred that my meal didn't still have eyeballs, but I made an exception this time. It was fresh and prepared wonderfully. This is how island life should be, not cold tuna out of a can.

THIRTEEN

It would have been nice to hang out there for a few days. Belize would be nice too, but I had an unwanted guest aboard and a primal urge to get back to where I considered home. Getting groceries was inconvenient, so we settled for topping off the water tanks. I talked the bartender into selling us a case of beer to go. He only charged us fifty-five bucks.

The good news was that now we could run at a good speed during the upcoming legs. There would be no idle speed dawdling to conserve fuel. The Belize and Mexico stops were civilized places with easy access to food, fuel, and booze. One little stop-over in Cuba and we'd be homeward bound. I sipped a beer and played with the GPS, parsing out alternatives, but found none. Each segment after Quintana Roo was nicely within our range and leaving a little reserve. Starr had figured it correctly.

We took off for San Pedro in the morning, which was on Ambergris Caye. My friend Holly and her partner, Tommy Thompson, had found sunken gold among the reefs just beyond the Mexican Border, near the Chinchorro Banks. They'd been stalked by some local thieves and enlisted Brody and me to help them recover it and not lose it to the bandits. We took *Leap of Faith* across to the Cayman Islands before returning to Florida. We could have made it all the way to Key West on fuel in that slow boat, but we didn't chance it. Starr and I got fuel in San Pedro and immediately returned to the sea.

After cruising past Holly's treasure hole and into Mexican waters, I zeroed in on a marina near Cozumel. Quintana Roo is technically the name of a Mexican State as opposed to a city. Cozumel is on an island off its coast. We pulled into Puerto de Abrigo with plenty of fuel to spare and topped off once again. There was still time to have a few cold ones before watching the sunset. We hit the bar for drinks and an update on the storm. We learned that instead of skirting the Keys, it had tracked across Cuba, where the mountains tore it apart. There was nothing left but some associated showers. Sea conditions in the Gulf were favorable. That news was celebrated with another dinner of fresh fish.

"Cuba then home," said Starr. "Florida is within our grasp."

"You still thinking about Fort Myers Beach?" I asked. "Or are you dropping off in Key West?"

"Are you still trying to get rid of me?"

"Just asking," I said.

"I'd love to talk you into staying in Key West for a bit," he said. "It is part of America, you know. We can do the Duvall Crawl and hit on the tourist girls."

"I'm going to get fuel in the Bight," I said. "It will be late afternoon by the time we get there. That will give you one night to play. I'll be running up the Northwest Channel the next morning."

"You're no fun," he said. "Only one night?"

"My mood isn't as playful as yours," I said. "No offense, but the sooner we part ways the better."

"That's some gratitude," he said.

"You're being paid," I countered. "Generously. If I'd have known about the canal agents in Panama, I could have made the trip without you."

"A man's got to do what a man's got to do."

"I understand that," I said. "That's why I've tolerated your presence. Besides, I would have had a tough time carrying all those fuel cans without you."

"That's right," he said. "You might still be stuck in Honduras."

"So tell me about this Cuban fuel stop."

"La Bajada," he said. "Not a damn thing there but a fuel depot for the Cuban Navy."

"How do we know we won't encounter a patrol boat?"

"We don't," he said. "But we can easily outrun them."

"Only until we run out of fuel," I said. "After we fill up, I won't care."

"The patrols work the North coast," he said. "From Havana and back again. They don't hang around on the west end because there is nothing there. Chances of seeing one are minimal."

"The one time I wandered into Cuban waters near there I saw one," I told him. "I also spent a few nights in custody on the other end of the island. I don't have fond memories of the place."

"Our arrival will make some poor bastard's day," he said. "We give him some real American money so he can feed his family. Consider it a noble cause, charitable even."

Back on the boat, I triple-checked the remaining distance to Key West. We could not make it on fuel. We had to make that stop in Cuba. My old trawler could run from Cozumel to Key West and back again without a fill-up, but she was no longer mine. I wondered where she was and how she was being treated. I hoped that her new owner was taking good care of her. *Miss Six* showed no ill-effects from running out of fuel. She had been running flawlessly, just sucking up the diesel like there was no tomorrow. As soon as we filled up in La Bajada, we'd get out of Cuban waters and continue for Key West. The timing wasn't quite right to get a slip in Key West Bight, but we could anchor off until morning as long as the weather was good.

There were grocery stores all over the place in Cozumel, so we filled our pantry and fridge with food. So many people spoke English that we could have been in America. Prices were high to jam the tourists, but that was the least of our worries. We were ready to begin the final run to Florida.

When we left Cozumel and ventured out into the strait that separated the Caribbean Sea from the Gulf of Mexico, the sea had some rollers left over from the storm. They weren't big breaking waves, just gentle mounds of water rising up and down. Once clear of any traffic, I eased the throttles forward and felt the surge of power that the Hatteras was capable of. The rollers didn't bother her at all. It wasn't long before we could make out the mountains of Cuba in front of us. We entered Bahia de Corrientes on the west end of the island and slowed to a crawl. I wanted to get a good look at what I was boating into. I used the binoculars to find the dock, with Starr's assistance. It was empty, so we proceeded with caution, constantly looking back for a patrol boat.

There was no one present when we pulled up to the dock. We put out fenders and eased alongside to tie up. Starr set off towards a little shack further up the hill. I heard him yell hello in Spanish a couple of times, before a bent and weathered Cuban gentleman appeared. He flashed some cash, and the man nodded in agreement. The two of them walked slowly back to the dock. I got off the boat to help with the hose because the old man didn't look capable. In fact, he looked like he was starving. I couldn't recall or never knew how to ask him if he would like something to eat.

"Quiero comida?" I asked. "Want food?"

He looked at me suspiciously, then at Starr.

"It's okay, man," Starr said. "Tenemos comida. We have food."

"Si," said the old man. "Podria comer."

We got the hose in the starboard tank, and our new friend got the pump running. I went inside and made the poor guy a ham sandwich. I grabbed a cold beer and handed the lunch over to the fuel attendant.

"Gracias," he said. "Muchas gracias."

Starr and I transferred the hose to the portside tank while the man ate. When our tanks were full, we wound up the hose for our new friend while he figured out the bill. We paid him in cash, then gave him an extra hundred for his troubles. He tried to turn it down, but I wouldn't have it.

"Salud," he said. "Salud, mi hijo."

I looked at Starr for a translation.

"He said bless you, my son," Starr said.

"Tell him that it's my honor."

"Es un honor," Starr said. "No problema."

The man looked past us out into the bay.

"Is there a patrol boat due?" I asked. "Bote patella?"

"Hoy," he said, turning to leave.

"Que hora," I asked. "What time?"

He shrugged and continued his slow walk to his shack.

"Let's get out of here," I told Starr. "Like, now."

I started both engines and Starr untied us. The old man was out of sight, probably sleeping off his sandwich and beer; dreaming up ways to spend his money. As soon as the boat was straightened out, I throttled her up hard. I wanted to make a quick exit before the expected patrol boat arrived. We sped across the bay towards the far northwest corner of the island. Before we made the point, and the open ocean, the Cuban Navy appeared. The gray gunboat was blocking the shortest route out of there, but the mouth of the bay was wide. I veered off to port and increased speed. *Miss Six* responded with glee. We ran at forty-five knots away from trouble. There wasn't much the Cubans could do, unless they wanted to fire on us.

They didn't even try to give chase, and no shots rang out. Once we were well clear, I made a big wide turn to the northwest and slowed down to cruising speed. That maneuver ate up much of our fuel reserve, but we still had enough to make it. I engaged the autopilot and let out a sigh of relief.

"What is it with you and Cuba?" Starr asked.

"I've got bad juju with that island," I said. "I tried to tell you."

"It's behind us now," he said. "Next stop, Key West."

I wasn't ready to celebrate quite yet. Cuba still loomed large off our starboard side. I shifted course slightly more north to put some distance between us and them. I aimed for a spot in the Florida Straits halfway between the Dry Tortugas and the Marquesas. Those waters were more familiar to me and would start to make me feel more at home. The sea was calm, the sky was blue, and *Miss Six* was singing her happy song as we zipped across the surface. I looked back at our wake and smiled. *Miss Leap* barely left a wake at all. Moving at this speed, in a boat this size was something to behold. I dismissed my concerns about her lousy fuel mileage momentarily and enjoyed the ride.

I'd been to Key West many times. Mostly I approached from the north; coming down the Northwest Channel and around Sunset Island and into the harbor. Sunset Island was once called Tank Island, but some developer bought it and built a fancy resort. Tank didn't fit any longer, so it was changed by the Key West Town Council to make it sound more palatable for tourists. Other times I'd come down Hawk Channel from Marathon, Islamorada, or Miami. I always anchored the old trawler and can confidently say that Key West is one of the worst places to stay at anchor out of all my travels. The bottom isn't great for holding anchors, and there is virtually no protection from the wind. The long dinghy ride to the Key West Bight is sometimes treacherous, and the dinghy dock itself is a pain in the ass. There are always more dinghies trying to tie up than there is room.

The clientele of the dinghy dock isn't exactly on the highest level either. Characters abound, from drug addicts, the mentally ill, to criminals and colorful people. I'd never had real trouble from any of them. They somehow mixed in with the cruisers and tourists in the menagerie that is Key West, but one always had to keep an eye out. I started thinking about ditching my passenger. He wanted to stay and play on Duval Street. Why not let him?

I couldn't shake the nagging feeling that he was trouble, although he'd done nothing to verify that suspicion. He helped with our little home invasion in Cartagena. He'd been useful getting in and out of strange fuel docks. He walked and even swam to help me carry fuel in Honduras. His resentment showed a couple of times, but I couldn't blame him for that. I'd stolen his home and livelihood. It may have been Captain Fred's call, but I was the one who carried out the repo. Not only had I taken the boat, but now it was mine. That had to stick in his craw. Under different circumstances, I may have considered him a good guy. Other than a lack of ambition, I couldn't find much fault.

Still, some sixth sense kept telling me to be wary. I tried to think like him. If I were going to kill the captain and steal his boat and money, the Florida Straits would be a good place to do it. The body would never be found. He could ditch the boat in the Keys somewhere, or possibly even sell it for a fraction of its value. The object of his scorn would be eliminated, and he'd have plenty of money to make a new start anywhere in the world. I talked myself into a fear of what he might try.

I had my pistol in a soft case on the dash. I reached for it, removing it from the case and tucking it between my back and the seat. After a few miles, I racked a round into the chamber. Starr was below getting us something to eat. He acted perfectly normal when he came back to the bridge with sandwiches. I made a sweeping turn to the east to run along the islands to the west of Key West. Many don't even realize that there are more islands out there. The Dry Tortugas are farthest out, and they are the most well-known. Seaplanes and ferries haul tourists out there every day the weather is good. The lesser-known islands, including the Marquesas, are much less visited. Locals with small boats run out there to party, and the occasional cruiser makes a stopover, but they are mostly empty.

These islands provide some great fishing for those willing to make the run, but the weather has to be perfect. At one time, it was common for fishermen to find Cuban refugees out here, but that type of traffic has been greatly reduced since the most recent change in our Cuban policy. The populace of Key West has a great affinity for the Cuban people and often welcomed refugees and rendered assistance rather than reporting them to the authorities. Most eventually made their way to Miami where they had relatives, but some stayed.

I couldn't help but like Key West, but I'd never want to live there. A day or two hitting the bars was all I could stand. The water was pretty, and the vibe was unique, but it wasn't for me. I didn't know if Starr was good enough with his guitar and singing to make it there, but I was becoming more and more convinced that it would be wise to part ways sooner rather than later. There was nothing that I needed him for any longer. I just had to figure out how to break the news to him without pissing him off. I mulled it over as we got closer and closer to Key West.

We were fine on fuel, so I didn't shortcut the turn north towards the harbor. I rounded the buoys for the main ship channel to stay in deep water. I kept up our speed until we passed Fort Zach on the far southwest corner of the island. There was a giant Disney boat at the cruise ship dock. Mickey Mouse greeted us as we passed by. It somehow seemed appropriate, though I'll never know why parents would want to take their children to this city. We passed by Mallory Square, but the sun had set hours earlier. Most of the revelers had left. We turned slightly to the northeast and passed by the Coast Guard Station, looking for a spot to anchor beside Fleming Key.

There was a small piece of mud near a jutting point that an anchor would grab into fairly well. It offered protection from an east wind only, but that was more protection than any other area offered. Two boats were already there, but there was enough room between them for me to drop anchor. It went smoothly, even in the dark. I was getting better with the new boat by the day. We had no dinghy so we couldn't get to shore, but that was fine by me. We still had beer, so I was content.

I took my gun to bed with me and secured the flimsy lock to my cabin door. I listened to Starr's movements, and couldn't go to sleep until after he went to bed. Dinghies and small boats returned to their motherships at all hours of the night. Their wakes made little waves that slapped the hull of the Hatteras. I felt exposed by all the traffic, and Starr's true intentions continued to bother me. I did not sleep well.

As soon as the marina office opened, I called them on the radio to request a slip for one night.

"One night?" asked Starr. "Come on, man, have a little fun."

"I'll give you the rest of your money now," I said. "Go to town and have all the fun you want."

Our slip was between Turtle Kraal's and the new Waterfront Brewery about halfway down the dock. There was no finger pier, so I had to back in to give us a way to get off the boat. Dozens of onlookers stopped to watch the pretty new boat. There is no current inside the break wall, and there was no wind that day. I slid her into her berth slicker than a buttered otter. There was a smattering of applause from the boardwalk.

"Good job, captain," Starr said. "You act like you've done that a time or two."

I climbed down and helped get us tied up properly before shutting down the engines. We still had a few hundred gallons of fuel, but I would need to fill up before leaving. We hooked up the water so we could both get a decent shower. Afterward, we walked the two blocks to Pepe's for a classic Key West breakfast.

FOURTEEN

Mac McAnally was sitting at another table with some people I didn't recognize. Starr wanted to harass him for an autograph. I suggested he let the man eat in peace.

"I wonder if Jimmy is in town too," he said, talking about Buffett.

"Who knows?" I replied. "Maybe they'll play an impromptu concert at Sloppy Joe's."

"I wouldn't want to miss that," he said. "We've got to stick around for a few days."

"We'll see," I said like I was talking to my kid. "But I can drink just fine without walking up Duval Street."

"You've got to loosen up, man," He said. "We're in the biggest adult playground in the country. Jimmy Buffett might be here. We've been through enough. Let's party."

"I tell you what," I began. "Let's go back to the boat and settle up with your money. Let me take it easy today. You go burn this fucker down if you want to. Maybe I'll come find you later."

"This place is like a candy store for big-league drinking," he said. "I can't decide where to go first."

"Michael McCloud starts in a few hours at Schooner's," I said. "Don't forget to pace yourself."

When we got back on the boat I made sure that all the money he had coming to him was in his pocket. He was practically salivating over the cash and his upcoming booze binge. I didn't have to ask him to leave. He was practically jogging towards Duval when I saw him last. I waited an hour before patrolling the waterfront. I didn't see him at any of the places that had a view of the Hatteras. I walked over to the fuel dock to check it out. It was an easy in and out, and it was currently unoccupied. I stuck my head in the office to let them know I was coming over for fuel. I asked for a hand tying up.

It was almost noon, so there were plenty of people around to watch me maneuver. I had no trouble at all, pulling out and around to the fuel dock. I looked around nervously for Starr as the diesel flowed. They had a high-speed pump, but it still took a while to transfer a thousand gallons. I tipped the attendant a twenty and asked him to hold me along the dock until I was ready. I climbed up to the bridge and fired her up again. There was no wind and no boats in my way, so I yelled for him to cut me loose. I backed up and turned around to leave the Bight.

Leaving Key West Bight to head north, you first have to go south a little bit to get around Sunset Island. From there you pick up the Northwest Channel which takes you about eight miles into the Gulf. There's a lot of activity at first, with fishing boats, parasailers and various tour boats traveling in every direction. I kept my wake to a minimum through all of that, but once I was clear, I laid the throttles down hard. *Miss Six* leaped forward with excitement. It wasn't the first time I'd cut loose her reins, but there was little stress in the situation, and it was the last leg of my journey. It felt fantastic.

There was something about Starr that I didn't trust. Now I was free of him. It was only one hundred and fifty miles to Fort Myers Beach. I was skimming along at over forty knots. I had a blue sea and blue skies, and I was almost home. I let the autopilot do its thing and went down to find the SAT phone. I dialed up Captain Fred; my friend, my benefactor, and now apparently my boss.

"Just a few hours out," I said. "Pick out a nice cut of meat for me."

"I've been aging some Wagyu Gold filets," he said. "Eight ounces of pure marbled goodness."

"I don't know what Wagyu is, but it sounds delicious," I said.

"Do I need one for your passenger?"

"Negatory," I said. "He doesn't know it yet, but I ditched him in Key West."

"A man who makes decisions and gets shit done," he said. "You can tell me all about it over a couple of Cubans. There's an empty slip on my starboard side. It's yours."

"Over and out, Kemosabe," I said.

Much of my weight had been lifted. I was damn near home. Whatever threat Starr presented had been neutralized. I had a big pile of cash stashed on a three million dollar yacht. Outside of Captain Fred, there was no one in the world depending on me for shit. I was a free man. I knew that I would also be a lonely man and that once I kicked back with nothing to do that it would all come back to me. The hurt wasn't gone. The loss would still be there, but I'd cross that bridge later. Today was a good day to be happy.

The approach to Fort Myers Beach was fairly straightforward. It was a due north course until you picked up the markers of Matanzas Pass. Bowditch Point created a big U-turn and marked the beginning of the no-wake zone. The first landmark after that was the Pink Shell Resort and Marina; home to Captain Fred aboard the Incognito V. All of his boats had been named Incognito. There was a brief time when he was in Punta Gorda, that folks mistook him for some Miami Dolphin football player of the same name. The guy was in trouble for bullying a teammate. I no longer followed the sport, so I never got the entire story. Anyway, Fred had people giving him the finger from the 41 bridge as they passed by and yelling nasty shit at him. One of his boats got blown up and burned right there at Pink Shell. Another got shot up pretty good by a Cuban helicopter hired by one of his enemies. He'd led an exciting life on those boats, and obviously a dangerous one. These days he had one of the world's most sophisticated security systems, and a team of men to help keep him safe. He'd directed his business acumen oversees on various projects that caused fewer issues with safety at home.

He was a true corporate titan, and I was extremely fortunate to call him my friend. Now he was about to cook me dinner. The tide was ripping in and threatened to screw up my docking pass, but I managed to adjust, and Fred was there waiting to grab lines along with two dockhands. We shook hands and gave each other a quick man-hug as soon as I set foot on the dock.

"Another success," he said. "I don't know how you do it but welcome back."

"Shit works out," I said. "It's good to be here."

"What's next for you?" he asked. "That's a lot of boat to just fart around in Pelican Bay."

"There's nothing I want to do more right now," I said. "I need to get a dinghy and maybe make a few adjustments, but I just want to float out there and be at peace."

"I'd forgotten how sharp looking this rig is," he said. "It suits you. Looks a little daring if you ask me. It's got some attitude."

"She served me well," I said. "But damn she drinks diesel like it's going through a fire hose."

"I ordered the biggest, most high-performance engines that Hatteras would put in her," he said. "Economy is rarely my concern."

"It was for the sap you hired to run charters with her," I said. "Said he couldn't turn a profit because of it."

"He got a free ride long enough," Fred said. "I've been thinking about her ownership. She's yours to do as you please, but it will stay in my name. If we transfer it legally, that might give you away. I'll keep the documentation up on it, but you'll have to stay in touch to keep your paperwork up to date."

"I've got no travel plans," I said. "What about you?"

"I'll be here for two more weeks," he said. "Then I've got some exploration to do in Costa Rica."

"Please don't ask me to run down there," I said. "I'll fly if you need me, but this boat isn't cut out for long-distance voyaging."

"I don't know what I'm getting into down there yet," he said. "I'll be listening to some pitches from people in the know. Now let's get you a beer. Tell me all about this Starr character."

We boarded Fred's yacht from the swim platform, passed through the lower stern area and up into the veranda where he had an outdoor kitchen. He handed me a longneck Landshark and a cigar. The wrapper said Perez Carillo.

"Not Cuban?" I asked.

"Rolled in the Dominican with Nicaraguan tobacco," he said. "Supposed to be the best on the planet. Cubans have been going downhill for a long time."

"Is there anything left that's good about that island?"

"I assume they still produce pretty young women," he said. "That's about it."

"Did I ever tell you about Yolanda?" I asked. We liked to tell each other stories.

"Cuban girl?" he asked. "I haven't heard that one."

"I got myself in a little jam down there one time," I began. "I had a relationship with a drug lord in the Keys, who also trafficked in Cubans from time to time. To win my freedom, I agreed to bring a young relative of a Cuban general back to the States on his behalf. Instead of delivering her to the kingpin in Tavernier, I ended up taking her all the way to Baltimore."

"Geez, why Baltimore?"

"She had some relatives there," I said. "I'm from the Chesapeake originally, so it was nice to go back for a brief visit."

"I've done business in Lagos," he said. "But you couldn't pay me to stay in Baltimore these days."

"Where haven't you done business?" I asked.

"North and South Poles," he said with a chuckle. "But as soon as they start developing, I'm there."

"The endless quest for victory," I said. "God knows you don't need the money."

"True, but the money is a most excellent side-effect," he said. "I've done some important things in my time, but I always wanted to be the best at something. That airport deal was pretty close, but it still wasn't enough. The tech wizardry that I came up with, well that should have been the capper to my career, but here I am still chasing windmills."

"Whatever makes you happy," I said. "More power to you."

"Power is just the thing, my boy," he said. "I was too ugly for politics, but I have skills in the boardroom and back alleys of the business world. I could buy those politicians. Some of them I have."

"I already know more about that than I need to," I said. "What kind of projects are you entertaining in Costa Rica?"

"This is what I find interesting," he said. "They want to remain at the forefront of eco-system protection, but they still need development. Balancing the two is very important to them. I'm going to listen to both sides. If I can help them with carbon sequestration or emissions reductions, then I'm in the door when they want to modernize the port in Limon or build new highways and bridges."

"Are you on board with all that global warming stuff?"

"Doesn't matter if I'm on board or not," he said. "It's what they want, and they're willing to spend to achieve their goals. If I can help them reforest land or build renewable energy plants, I will; as long as I'm getting richer in the process."

"What's your endgame there?"

"Limon," he said. "They will eventually spend billions to turn that port into a world-class facility. They'll need to upgrade water and sewer to the city in the process. An integrated infrastructure project that is well within my expertise and experience."

"So if you plant enough trees and build enough solar and wind farms you'll get that deal," I said.

"That's the plan."

"Sounds pretty smart to me," I said.

"I didn't get here by being a dumbass," he said. "Anytime you want a position with any of my holdings, just say the word."

"I think you know better than that," I said. "No way I could reenter the corporate world."

"Just throwing it out there," he said. "If times ever get too rough, you've got a fallback plan."

"I appreciate it," I said. "But I'm hoping to drop dead on that boat or a beach, about forty years from now."

"I'm planning on being shot down by some young hottie's husband," he said. "I'll be coming and going at the same time."

"Sounds about right," I said.

"So what's next for you?" he asked. "I mean in the short term before you retire to a life of leisure."

"I need a dinghy or small boat to run back and forth in for starters," I said. "And an inverter. Maybe additional batteries. That thing has every cool gizmo available but no inverter. Watermaker, ice machine, night vision, fire suppression, bow thruster, air conditioning out the wazoo; but no inverter. I want to make a cup of coffee without running a 20kw Onan to do it."

"Most folks would be plugged in at a marina," he said. "Normal people."

"This is real nice," I said. "But I won't be able to deal with it for long. Look at that traffic going across the bridge. Look at all these people everywhere."

"I go inside and ignore all that," he said. "Keeps me out of the heat too."

"After a year in the mountains the heat feels pretty good," I replied.

"Wait until you get to be my age," he said. "You'll find a way to pay for a marina slip and set the a/c at seventy. Now let me start those steaks. Grab yourself another beer."

The filets were unbelievable. They had a buttery flavor, and you could cut them with a fork. Fred was quite proud of himself. He had prepared them perfectly. When I left the table, I went down one level to light up the cigar he'd given me. It had a rich aroma and a tangy citrus finish. I was no expert, but I thought it was damn good. Fred just chewed on his without lighting it, as was his habit. I never understood paying ten or twelve bucks for a good cigar and not smoking it but to each his own.

We never got around to discussing Jim Starr. Somewhere in the middle of a dissertation on politics in Colombia, I started to fall asleep. I begged off and returned to my own Hatteras for the night. I'd forgotten to turn the air on, and it was hot and muggy inside. I cranked up my array of air conditioners, and it was cool in about five minutes. I locked the outer doors and put my gun on the nightstand in the master berth. I was out of it before my head hit the pillow. It had been a long few weeks, but now I could finally rest.

I was not disturbed by outside forces, but my dreams were disconcerting. I saw vague images of a man. I couldn't identify him. I saw Brody giving me a look that I couldn't interpret. Each new image raised more questions in my mind. I kept waiting for the dream sequence to reveal what I should do, but it never happened. I was still confused about it when I woke up the next morning. The sun was well up into the sky. I'd slept much later than usual. I was still a little foggy when I took my coffee out to the cockpit to watch the passing boats. A fisherman went by on a little Hewes Redfisher. I liked it a lot. I thought maybe that would make a good tender for the Hatteras. I could fish, but I could also use it to run to town for groceries or other supplies.

I had no way to hoist or store the thing though. I'd have to tow it behind the big boat and leave it in the water all the time. The more I thought about the idea, the more I believed it would be a good solution. Flats boats were fast, and I could be where I needed to go in a hurry, without burning a hundred gallons per hour. I wanted to find something similar to the one I'd just seen, but of course, I had no internet. I was also hungry again. I had no breakfast foods that suited me, so after a second cup of coffee, I walked Estero Boulevard to the Lighthouse Tiki

Bar. They served halfway decent fare and were far enough off the beach to discourage tourists.

I listened to the chatter of my fellow patrons and took in the atmosphere. It was quite unlike any place in the mountains. Everyone wore shorts and flip flops. There was no talk of snowfall or bear sightings. The mood was light, and most everyone was smiling. I had no desire to carry on a conversation with anyone, but the easy-going feel of the place was contagious. It was good to be out of the third world, and the mountains seemed very far away.

Later in the day, I told Fred about my flats boat idea. He directed me to his computer station and suggested some websites for local boat sales. The type of small vessels I was looking for were quite popular in Florida, so there were several available that appeared to be in good shape. I found an eighteen-footer right in Fort Myers Beach that fit the bill perfectly. It was well-appointed with dual power poles, poling platform, trolling motor, and trim tabs. It had a Yamaha 115 four-stroke and was only a few years old. The price was high in my estimation until I searched for others in the same class. The seller's market was good for these boats apparently.

I wanted it, but I had to work out a few logistical problems first. How would I get it to my big boat? What would I do with the trailer that came with it? What about the title transfer and registration? I didn't need that transaction pinpointing my location for some unknown threat that could track me down. I could pay cash, but the boat had to be legal, or the FWC would nail me every time I used it. Then I remembered that I had a crappy, old SUV parked at the marina. I'd forgotten all about it. I never followed through with the paperwork. The temporary tags would expire soon. I needed to get rid of it, but maybe I could use it to haul my new boat to a ramp after I bought it.

I grabbed the keys to the thing and went out to the parking lot. The battery was dead and one tire was flat. I went back to disturb Fred and discuss my issues.

"I'll have my lawyer handle the transfer," he said. "We'll put it in one of my company names. I'll get Triple-A out here to get that jalopy going. Go get your boat and don't worry about the details."

"What about the trailer it comes on?" I asked.

"Leave it at a busy boat ramp," he said. "Someone will steal it eventually. Then it's their problem."

"Easy enough," I said. "I'll bring you the title once I seal the deal."

"Do it quick," he said. "I'll be leaving for Costa Rica, and I don't know how long I'll be gone."

"Not a problem."

FIFTEEN

The owner of the flats boat was named Ted Bush. His phone voice had a high country note to it. I asked if he was from the mountains.

"If you count Kentucky," he said. "Came here to avoid ever seeing snow again, and to fish to my heart's delight."

"Why you selling her?"

"It started with all that bad water and Red Tide last year," he said. "There was no point in even trying to find a fish around here. Water quality is much better now, but the fishing isn't the same."

"What will you do with your free time now?"

"I've got some inland hobbies," he said. "Gun sports and archery. There are ranges on every other street corner in this state."

"You can buy a lot of range time with what you're asking."

"It's a fair price," he said. "Nary a scratch on her and she comes with all the toys. I've put maybe five-hundred hours on the motor. I can't justify letting it sit in the driveway and not get used."

"Bring the titles with you," I said. "I've got the cash."

Ted Bush lived at the south end of Estero Island. We agreed to meet at the closest boat ramp to his place, which was on Lover's Key. I had him launch the boat, so I could take it for a quick test drive. We tied up at a side pier and did the deal in the parking lot. He unhooked the trailer, and we shook hands. He seemed pleased with his new wad of bills. He signed the seller's portion of the boat and trailer titles and gave me a handwritten bill of sale. I wouldn't need the title to the trailer. It stayed right where he left it.

The ramp was on Estero Bay. I had some skinny water to run through to get back up to the Pink Shell Marina, but that's what flats boats were built for. The trip was less than ten miles, and I was back at my boat in thirty minutes. Without the no-wake zone through the mooring field, I could have made it in fifteen. The Yamaha ran smoothly, and the little boat handled well. It did indeed have all the gadgets a man could think to buy for a small boat. I liked it. I liked it a lot. It was a huge step up from an inflatable dinghy. I was going to need some fenders to keep it from banging the Hatteras, and some cans for extra fuel, but that was about it.

I gave the boat title to Captain Fred, and he promised to hand it off to one of his lawyers. The current registration sticker was good for another six months. I couldn't wait to bother the redfish and snook in Pelican Bay with my new toy. Using it to run for supplies would also save me from burning all that fuel in the Hatteras every time I needed more beer.

Fred was busy on the phone planning the details of his Costa Rica trip, but he made some time to engage me in an important discussion concerning the terrible events that happened back in Banner Elk. I was anxious to learn what he'd found out. I was also anxious to disappear with both of my new boats. There was a chance that what he told me might put that on hold. If I had a clear target to pursue, I'd have to go after him, or her. If I survived my mission for revenge, the boats would be waiting for me when I got back. I have to admit that the searing passion to destroy her killer had faded somewhat, but I owed both her and myself justice.

"I dug pretty deep into this nonsense," he said. "Can't say that I've arrived at the heart of the matter, but I had to practically go all the way to Trump himself."

"Does that mean it was the FBI?" I asked.

"It seems like the most likely possibility," he said. "There is zero evidence that it involved any of your misadventures in the mountains."

"What evidence is there that it was the Feds?"

"Scant to little," he said. "There's been a big shakeup at the Bureau as you probably are aware. They've got a lot on their plate these days, and most of it involves covering up all the bullshit they've been involved in over the past several years."

"So what do we know?"

"I still have a line to the Senate Select Committee on Intelligence," he said. "That's made up of mostly the same players. All I have to go on is a vague suggestion that I look to the FBI. Brody's death is insignificant to them considering everything else that's taken place. A minor housekeeping task."

"Was the hit directed at her alone, or was I also a target?"

"I don't believe you were the primary target," he said. "But you witnessed her assassination. You were supposed to die too, son."

"What about now?" I asked. "Will they still come after me?"

"You are way down on their list of priorities," he said. "Almost nonexistent, but given an easy opportunity, they would neutralize you."

"So it was the right thing to vanish," I said. "And to cover my tracks."

"Most certainly," he said. "Do you know the name, David Bowditch?"

"I do," I said.

"He was hovering just below the top echelon when Comey and McCabe got fired," he said. "Wray got the top job, and Bowditch gets bumped up to second."

"So he's part of the old cabal," I said. "Still doing the dirty work even though he's now in the spotlight."

"But he hasn't been in the spotlight," Fred said. "Hardly anyone knows he exists, unlike McCabe. I have reason to believe that he's behind the hit. The shooter was not FBI though. He was a hired stooge, maybe a previous informant but not a professional."

"And he's quite dead," I said. "Convenient, isn't it?"

"Thanks to you."

"Brody and Bowditch were once a couple," I said. "He came to our cabin and helped us clear up a little mess. It was then that I learned of their previous relationship."

"Boat bum Meade Breeze," he said. "Friend of international businessman Fred Ford and enemy of the powerful in Washington. You are some kind of unique individual."

"I earned your friendship," I said. "You think Bowditch's efforts were an act of jealousy?"

"Why not kill you then, and leave Brody alive?"

"Unprofessional shooter with an automatic weapon," I said. "Figured he'd kill everyone at the scene and be done with it."

"I wish I could have discovered more," he said. "But you and Brody are not on anyone's radar. No offense, but I can't see them tracking you down now. Too much risk with too little reward. Stay invisible. Don't give them a reason to change priorities."

"It would be impossible to go after Bowditch without bringing down the wrath of the Bureau," I said.

"And everything I've told you is unconfirmed speculation on the part of senators who may or may not have an agenda that I don't know about. It's not worth acting on without corroboration. Better to be a ghost. That's my heartfelt advice to you."

"I'm sure it's sound advice," I said. "You're the smartest man I've ever met, but I don't like the taste of it. I ought to be able to do something."

"Sometimes discretion is the better part of valor," he said. "Stay alive to fight another day."

"I want peace," I said. "But at the same time, I want violence. Peace for myself and violence for whoever killed Brody."

"That's emotion talking and not good common sense," he said. "If you can't fight city hall you sure as hell can't fight the FBI."

"So what do I do now?"

"Grief is in two parts," he said. "The first is loss. The second is the remaking of life. That's you, Breeze. Your life is still in front of you."

He made good sense, but if I listened to him, it meant giving up on revenge. There would be no justice for Brody. The thought of that made me an angry man. The world had always been unjust. Life isn't fair, I knew that, but this time it had hit me and knocked me down. It backed up and ran over me again and again. I was supposed to accept that there was nothing I could do to make things right. I wasn't ready to come to terms with that, but what else could I do?

The time that I'd spent out of the country wasn't spent dwelling on my grief or Brody's death. Thanks to Captain Fred, I had been preoccupied with other things. A new boat, the previous captain, a politician in Cartagena, and all the challenges before me. Now those distractions had been removed. I was on the brink of a new life, but I was reluctant to let the past go. I had always told myself to never look back, and it had served me well. It could not apply to Brody. I couldn't not think about her. I couldn't stop my quest to avenge her, or could I? So far, I hadn't done a damn thing. I did return briefly to Banner Elk, but instead of taking any real action, I'd banged her only friend. Smooth move, Breeze. Maybe you're not the virtuous person you envisioned yourself to be. Maybe you deserved what karma had dished out after all.

I looked at my only remaining friend and saw concern in his eyes. I'd come to him for refuge and assistance, and he'd given me both. He'd gone above and beyond to take care of me and help me. The value of his counsel was immeasurable. The value of his friendship even more so. The value of the boat he'd given me was somewhere close to three million dollars.

"You're right," I said. "I've got to drop it if I want to survive."

"I want you to survive if that means anything to you."

"It does," I said. "It means a lot. You know that."

"You've got that flats boat now," he said. "Get on out of here and rest your soul. Go be at peace."

"I still need to get an inverter," I said. "I haven't figured out who to hire for that."

"It can wait," he said. "I've got to fly out the day after tomorrow. Go anchor up in some quiet cove for a while. When you come back, we'll get you outfitted with whatever you need."

"That sounds nice," I said. "That's what I really want to do."

"Then go do it."

He was right. I was delaying for no particular reason. It was what I wanted, but I'd put it off. Now was the time to go. I could survive without an inverter or solar panels or more batteries just like I'd done on the way back from Panama. Twelve hundred gallons of fuel would run the generator for a long time. It was pretty quiet and wouldn't disturb the peace of Pelican Bay. I could run it for a few hours every day to keep the batteries charged, make coffee, and even run the air conditioning if I felt like it. I needed to accept what an awesome gift it was and use it to its full potential. I also had the Redfisher, it would make things easier and more fun. There was a life out there for me; the life I wanted. There was no more reason to hang around, wishing for some way to enact revenge on some mysterious figure that I'd never meet. It was time for me to go.

"My phone is on around the clock," Fred said. "It's beyond the eyes of Apple, Google, or the NSA. You can reach me anytime."

"I'll try not to disturb you while you're reconfiguring the economy of Costa Rica," I said. "But it would be nice to come visit when you get back."

"A few weeks or maybe a month," he said. "Keep in touch."

I made sure that *Miss Six* was locked up and secured. I checked on the Redfisher too, before walking a few blocks to the Upper Deck above the Matanzas Inn. It was Scotty Bryan's night to play. I climbed the stairs, and sure enough there he was. He saw me enter and acknowledged me. His next song was The Cape, by Guy Clark.

"He's one of those who knows that life is just a leap of faith,

Spread your arms and hold your breath,

Always trust your cape."

I looked around for Jennifer, but she wasn't behind the bar or waiting tables. I ordered a pizza and guzzled the first beer. Other than Scotty, I didn't recognize anyone. The crowd had changed since I'd been here last. From the Upper Deck, you can see the car traffic on the bridge and the boat traffic underneath of it. I looked out over the mooring field and remembered how many times I'd seen my old trawler out there. I wondered if any of my old friends were still around. The Three Amigos of the backwater had accepted me when I had nothing. In return, I had paid Diver Dan and Robin big bucks to help me run dope in the Keys. I'd rescued One-legged Beth from drug addiction and helped her to start a new life up the river in Fort Myers. None of them had a damn thing except a boat to live on, but they'd help any neighbor who needed it.

I ate and drank more than my fill. Scotty had a table full of willing tourists making requests. It didn't matter the song, he knew it and could do a decent job of it. He was best at songs from long ago, the kind that rarely comes on the radio anymore, but bring back good memories. He was starting a Jim Croce tune as I was leaving. I dropped a ten in his tip jar and thanked him.

"Don't be a stranger," he said, before launching into Croce's *Operator.*

I walked down Crescent Street until it came to Estero Boulevard, just a block from the liquor store. To my surprise and chagrin, it was closed. I knew it didn't fail as a business. The place was always busy. Some developer must have bought them out. It was prime beachfront real estate. I turned around and went back two blocks to Nick's Discount Liquor. I knew from past experience that the prices were anything but a discount, but saving a buck wasn't my highest priority. I got an overpriced bottle of rum and carried it back to the boat.

I made a mental checklist of things to do. I needed groceries and a little spare gas. I could get diesel and water at Moss Marine on the way out. I needed cases and cases of beer. I still had my jalopy SUV, which I could use to run errands, but I needed to dispose of it sooner rather than later. I hadn't transferred the title to the thing, but I couldn't leave it on the street. I wanted it crushed into a small cube and recycled so it would never be found. There was a salvage yard on San Carlos Boulevard about a mile onto the mainland. I could drop it off and walk back.

The rum wasn't the best, but it served the purpose. Pink Shell was away from the rowdier parts of the beach and attracted a somewhat affluent customer. I sat in peace and thought of how far I'd come. I was back to being a boat bum, but this time, I was doing it in style.

When the heat or mosquitoes drove me inside, I could crank up the generator, turn on the air conditioning, and make ice for my rum. I could even make water now. I could take more regular showers too. If I got bored, I could take my new flats boat to town for drinks or a decent meal. I was looking forward to it. I just needed to finish my errands first.

The next day I drove all over the place to get food and beverages. Traffic through the beach was at its usual crawl, but I managed to fill the boat with food and booze. I got a couple of gas cans from NAPA. I filled up the cans and the Redfisher at Moss Marine, which made me thirsty. I took the little boat over to Bonita Bill's for some cheap beer. It was a local's hangout with greasy food and daily specials that attracted those with less cash to spend. As soon as I stepped foot on the dock, I heard my name being called. I looked around for someone that I knew.

"Breeze, it's me, over here."

I'll be damned if it wasn't One-legged Beth behind the bar.

"Where the hell have you been?" she said.

"In the mountains," I said. "Believe it or not. I thought you were up in the city."

"I didn't like some of the folks anchored up there," she said. "Some of them didn't like me."

"Welcome back to both of us," I said. "You doing all right?"

"Making ends meet," she said. "I'm only working two days a week. I still get my disability. You staying long?"

"Trying to get out of here, to be honest with you," I said. "But I'll be around."

"Where's your boat?"

Don't get me wrong, I liked Beth, but something told me not to tell her too much. She didn't know what kind of boat I had now and she didn't need to know.

"In a marina," I said. "Probably leaving tomorrow."

"Don't be a stranger," she said.

It was the second time I'd heard that in twenty-four hours. I could complete the trifecta by riding out to the backwater to find Diver Dan or Robin. I sat in a far corner and tried to think of anything I'd missed. As far as I could tell, I was ready. I checked the "free wall" where liveaboards would leave stuff they didn't want any more, but others might be able to use. Sometimes Bonita Bill's would have day-old bread or pastries for those in need. Occasionally they held nautical swap meets. The place was on the opposite end of the wealth spectrum from the Pink Shell. It was closer to my roots, but no one there needed to know what kind of boat I had now. I'd probably be banished forever. I left Beth a twenty-dollar tip on a ten-dollar tab and took off.

I was starting to realize that my big step up in the boating hierarchy might cause some resentment amongst the old gang. It certainly wasn't beneath me to associate with them now, but I wasn't sure how they'd take my good fortune. I couldn't afford to hobnob with people who owned boats like mine, but my place was no longer in the backwater swatting mosquitoes and picking up day-old bread from Bonita Bill's. I was an imposter among the rich, but too wealthy for the poor. I would deal with it. I'd never fit in anywhere for most of my life. Being alone in the world was nothing new, but I'd had a good break from it with Brody.

She had encouraged me to expand my horizons and shown me how to open up to another human being. I would do anything for her, not to simply make her happy, but to make us both happy. She killed the loneliness within me, at least for a time. I was about to experience it all over again. I wanted it, as a matter of fact. It was what I knew and was most comfortable with. It wasn't so much Breeze against the world, but more like Breeze by himself and to hell with the rest of the world. Anytime I was exposed to what was taking place in modern society; it repelled me.

Modern culture had left me far behind. I didn't understand any of it. Music sucked. Government on all levels was incompetent. Sexuality of all sorts was in your face everywhere you turned. Right was wrong, and wrong was right. Up was down and down was up. It made my head spin even in small doses. I was much better off on some beach alone, searching for snook in the surf. I knew where the sun rose and where it set. That was good enough for me, but I doubted most folks today could point to where either happened at their house.

I couldn't know how many years I had left, but I wouldn't spend it attempting to conform to standards I couldn't accept. I just didn't belong there. Now it seemed like I didn't belong with the few other boat bums I'd known. If the only place for me was by myself, then so be it. I'd talk to the manatees when I needed some conversation. It was time to leave Fort Myers Beach. Fred was off to Costa Rica. I had my small boat and plenty of supplies. I'd come to Florida for this. There was no reason to put it off any longer.

Sixteen

Moss Marine's docks had been wiped out during Hurricane Irma. The newly built floating docks were a huge improvement, but I only cared about getting diesel. It was convenient to the Gulf or ICW and an easy in and out. I timed my fuel stop for the slack tide to make things easier. The dockhands were helpful and friendly. It was the last thing I needed before my final departure. I idled away with full tanks and rounded Bowditch Point. There were no boats in my way, so I hammered the throttles down and raced out into the Gulf at top speed. I followed the marked channel out to deep water before turning to run along the coast of Sanibel and eventually heading north. It's only twenty-five miles to the entrance to Boca Grande Pass from Point Ybel. I was there in forty-five minutes. I kept my speed through the Pass until I approached the entrance to

Pelican Bay, keeping an eye on the flats boat I towed behind me.

Cayo Costa was off my starboard side in all her glory. Small boats dotted the sandbar at the entrance. Dogs ran along the shore while their owners drank beer waist-deep in the water. I couldn't believe how fast I'd gotten here. In the old days, it was an all-day trip. Now it took an hour. I slowed to a crawl and passed the park service docks. I took a peek into Manatee Cove but decided to anchor behind the bar on the Punta Blanca side of the bay. I'd left my rum still hidden in the mangroves there a long time ago. I had no use for it now, but it would be cool to see if it was still there.

I'd also grown dope on Cayo Costa back then. Once I had a pound or so, I'd take it up to Punta Gorda to sell to suburban housewives. It kept me afloat, so to speak. I sold my home-made rum to bums in the park until they decided they could gang up on me and take the rum for free. It seemed like a million years ago. I had to make those sales to buy food and fuel, or I wouldn't survive. Somehow I parlayed that into multiple pound shipments to the Keys, and eventually pickups of huge bales from the

Tortugas. I scratched and clawed out a living, never knowing when it would all end. I hid from the FBI and the IRS until one day, it all came crashing down. I had a nice cash fund built up, which only served to get me out of jail and pay off my debts. I started back at zero after that.

This time was different. I didn't need to sell dope or rot-gut rum. I had money. I had a fabulous boat. I wasn't wanted by the law for any crimes I'd committed. I may have been on someone's hit list in Washington, D.C., but I was by no means a priority. If I stayed clean and avoided contact with law enforcement, they would never know where I was. That part was just like old times. I laughed at the thought of the collective intelligence of the FBI not being able to find me. It was only Brody who finally tracked me down after she had taken a sabbatical from her job as an agent. She figured out that I was not only low-tech but no tech. She put herself in a boat and spent many hours and days living a life like mine, in the places I was known to travel. She didn't use computers to access ATM records, license plate readers, or traffic cameras. She went old school. She was gone now. She'd been the only one smart enough to find me. They wouldn't have a clue without her.

I slowed to a crawl through a narrow cut between a long sand bar to my port and grass flats to my starboard. The entrance carried six feet of water at dead low tide. Beyond it was mostly eight feet deep with a good sand bottom as long as you stayed away from seagrass. I used to hide often in a dead-end cove at the back of the bay, but it was buggy in the summertime. I chose an open water spot roughly in the middle. I stopped the boat and climbed down quickly to grab the flats boat before it bashed into the hull of the Hatteras. I let the big boat float freely while I tied the skiff off to the side. I ran back up and put it in reverse, dropping the anchor at the same time. Once I had enough chain out, I let things settle down before reversing again to dig the anchor in. It held firmly, promising to provide a good night's sleep and security in a storm.

I was home. I stood up on the bridge and looked around. A dolphin rose to say hello. Ospreys circled above looking for mullet. I shut down the engines and got myself a beer. I took a seat in the fighting chair that probably cost as much as a new car. After the first beer, I visited the engine room to look for signs of leaks or active drips. It was hot down there, but there was plenty of room and light for the inspection. Everything was still clean and dry, which amazed me. The bilge area on *Leap of Faith* had eventually evolved into a toxic wasteland from saltwater, oil and other fluids. I could eat off the floor in the engine room of *Miss Six*.

I came out sweaty and even thirstier. Beer number two disappeared in ten seconds. Beer number three took a little longer. I sat down again and surveyed the surrounding waters and mangrove shorelines. The entrance I had used was the only way in, so any approaching vessel would be noticed. There was nowhere to go from here except back out. No boats would be casually passing by on their way to someplace else. Only captains with good local knowledge would know how to get through the cut. It was a great choice. The natural landscape provided a certain element of security.

It was hot, but the afternoon sea breeze was kicking in. I decided to take an inventory of the fishing tackle onboard. Most of it was suitable for marlin and tuna, but I did find a nice little light tackle outfit that would do adequately for snook and redfish. I had to dig deep to find small lures that would work on the local fish population. That was one thing I'd forgotten. I put it on my list for when I needed to run to town for more beer. I threw the rod, some jig heads and soft plastics in the Redfisher and fired her up. I cruised over to Murdock Bayou just to feel the wind in my hair and to stretch the little boat's legs. I deployed the trolling motor and started working a thick stand of mangroves that overhung deeper water. Gamefish in Florida sought shade in the heat of the day. Early mornings were best. Mid-afternoons were tough. It took two hours, but I finally pulled a keeper redfish out of some sunken pilings where a dock used to be. He went in the fish box to be consumed later.

Having procured my dinner, I decided to head over to Cabbage Key. I paid four bucks for a can of beer and checked out the wait staff and bartenders. They were all way too young to think about hitting on. I'd been able to attract some women younger than me over the years, but these girls looked like teenagers. I left a dollar tip and walked down to the docks. Several dinghies were beached on the shore to my left. They were likely from cruising boats anchored nearby, either in Pelican Bay or off Useppa Island.

I drove a brief stretch of the ICW before veering off and using the back entrance to Pelican Bay. It wasn't deep enough for the Hatteras but was fine for smaller vessels. I cruised slowly into Manatee Cove and shut down the motor. Soon enough, I saw several manatees come up to breathe. They weren't bothered by my presence. I watched for fifteen minutes, glad to know that some things never change. I cruised along the shore past the park service docks. The big ferry dock had been badly damaged by Irma but was now repaired. Park rangers kept a watchful eye on visitors to the island. No one got by them without paying the requisite two-dollar fee. I was out of small bills, so I gave it a pass. I added that to my list too. I needed to break up a bunch of hundred dollar bills.

I was reminded of all the cash I had stored on the boat and started to worry over it. I went back, fileted my catch and put the meat on ice. After washing up, I pulled out all the money and spread it out over the countertop between the galley and the salon. Add all the weapons I was carrying, and I could easily be mistaken for a drug dealer. Captain Fred knew about all this cash, and so did Jim Starr. I could trust Fred; Starr, not so much. His eagerness to party it up in Key West was a stroke of luck. Getting rid of him eased my mind and calmed that niggling feeling in my gut. My only worry was the random stranger boarding my boat in my absence. If I was gone for too long, it would be a tempting target. Taking the small boat to get groceries and supplies would leave it vulnerable until I returned. I never used to worry about that sort of thing, but the old trawler didn't suggest wealth. The Hatteras screamed money.

I had to laugh at myself. In one day I'd made of mess of the interior of my fancy new boat. Fishing tackle was strung everywhere, and guns and money lined the counter. I needed to organize and protect all of it. Without the coolness of air conditioning, humidity and salt would get to everything. My first step was to crank up the generator and turn on all the cooling units. Then I split the cash into smaller bundles and used Ziplock bags to keep it dry. I studied the interior for places to hide it. It wouldn't take much to frustrate an opportunistic thief that just happened to be passing by, but if Starr ever found me; he knew this boat better than I did.

I put it off and picked out strategic placement for my guns. I wished I had some gun oil to keep them from rusting. I added that to the list. Then I wasted some freshwater cleaning all the fishing gear and stowing it neatly. I went back to the money. I stared at the stacks of bills, realizing that I was hungry. I cooked up half the redfish and chased my meal with yet another beer. At this rate, I would need to replenish my supply every three or four days. I felt better after eating and started stashing twenty grand here and twenty grand there. Some went in the engine room, some up on the bridge, some in various nooks and crannies in the interior, and some in various compartments hidden under tools or tackle. It wasn't the perfect solution, but if I got robbed, I'd likely only lose a tiny portion of the total. If a thief found twenty grand, he'd be overjoyed and ready to split.

I already had a to-do list. I needed small bills. I needed fishing stuff. I needed gun oil, and I was out of Ziplock bags. Half a case of beer had vanished. I had the generator running fulltime, and I wondered how long the diesel would last. I had to make sure I had enough to make it to a fuel dock. I couldn't run it until the tanks were empty. I figured the thousand gallons I had left would last quite a while. Day one was finished. The sun was about to go down over the mangroves of Cayo Costa, so I went outside to admire it.

There were a few boats anchored near the main entrance to Pelican Bay, close to the Boca Grande Pass, but I couldn't see them from where I was. Nothing disturbed my view of the sun. The fishermen and day boaters had all gone home. I was alone; isolated from everything but this moment. I did a shot of rum in honor of the sun and asked it to please come back tomorrow. Then I ran inside to avoid an onslaught of mosquitoes.

It was a quite pleasant seventy-four degrees in the luxurious salon of my fifty-four foot Hatteras. I shook my head in disbelief. I thought it would be a good time to do some reading, but I had no books. I added it to the list. It felt much the same as it had in the past, but at the same time, much was different. I loved it here, but sometimes it was a struggle.

The heat and the bugs and the lack of any conveniences beat you down. I had no choice but to endure it previously, but now I was beyond comfortable. The Redfisher was a big step up from an inflatable dinghy, so I was more mobile. I had air conditioning, as long as the fuel lasted. I had plush leather to sit on and a big walk-around bed to sleep on. I was chilling like a villain. So why did I feel guilty about it?

It all boiled down to Brody. I hadn't acted honorably after the smoke cleared. I feared for my life so much that I'd abandoned her body and left her to the care of strangers. I dumped the cabin like a bad habit. I ran and hid and ran some more. I was no longer running, but I was still hiding. It took a long time to convince myself that there was nothing else I could have done. I'd put a bullet in the forehead of her killer. I'd saved my own life, which had to be worth something. Getting killed would have served no purpose, no matter how honorably my death took place.

I was still alive, and that's what had to matter now. I had the means and wherewithal to continue to survive off the grid. I could properly mourn her loss. I could lie down on the floor and bawl my eyes out, but I could also live. I should be able to continue to survive with the tiny chance that someday, her killer would be introduced to justice; Breeze justice.

I took a large swig of rum right out of the bottle, turned out the lights, and went to bed. The sheets were clean and cozy. I even had a washer and dryer on board. I needed to learn to appreciate all that I'd been given, in spite of my grief. Somehow, I needed to reconcile the paradox of great gain coming so soon after horrible loss.

I recalled my conversation with Starr about karma and all that I'd been taught in the churches of my youth. My earthly faith was that shit would work out. My faith about a future life, one after death, was less solid, but I knew that Brody was a soul. I saw her soul; touched it so to speak. That was something that I could have faith in. I'd have to be content with that and know that my sense of loss wouldn't suddenly disappear one day. Her memory would be with me as I sought to scratch out some measure of happiness in her absence.

I closed the book on the first real day of my new life. I put my head on the pillow, somewhat convinced that I would be okay. I touched the cold steel of the pistol on the nightstand to reassure myself that I'd be safe. This little chunk of the universe was mine. I felt secure here. Happiness would come or it wouldn't, but I intended to live long enough to find out.

SEVENTEEN

I set out to establish a new routine for myself. I wanted to be fit in both mind and body. I began by walking across Cayo Costa each morning and swimming in the Gulf. I briefly considered swimming off the boat in the bay but was reminded of catching bull sharks while tarpon fishing with a young Marine named Daniel. We fought several big enough to kill a man over a three day period. It ruined me for swimming in Pelican Bay forever. On the Gulf side, the water was clear, and visibility was excellent. The big predators hung out in the deep waters of the Boca Grande Pass and the darker inland waters with plenty of prey available. I'd rarely seen one in the surf.

I swam until I was worn out, then jogged on the beach; pushing myself a little harder each day. In all of my activities, I concentrated on redeveloping my keen sense of awareness. I tried to see everything that was happening around me, no matter how insignificant. I watched the sky for signs of changing weather. I watched the water for marine life, studying the habits of the creatures that lived in the bay. I focused on passing boats, noting the occupants and sorting them by threat level.

For a little extra stimulation, sometimes I visited the sand spit at the entrance to the bay where weekenders gathered to play in the sand and water. I beached my little boat where the music was good and observed the people; making up backstories in my head for each of them. I decided who worked with their backs and who worked with their brains. I guessed at which women held jobs and which stayed home to take care of the kids. I dubbed the loud-mouths assholes and the gentlemen good guys. I took note of pretty ladies in revealing bikinis, for research purposes, of course.

Whenever a kid would fish from shore, I'd offer tips and guidance. I'd pick up stray balls and Frisbees to toss for someone's dog. I blended in naturally, all the while keeping a wary eye on everyone. It was practice for the unknown time when certain skills would be necessary for survival. I worked to make it a habit; a second nature that could save my skin someday.

I was getting myself into decent shape again. Hiking in the mountains and chopping wood offered its challenges, but I'd been neglecting true fitness. I started doing pushups and sit-ups whenever I got bored. I soon learned that I couldn't do as many as I had a few years prior. I resolved to get back to that level and ignore the fact that I'd aged since then. I limited myself to six beers per day with the occasional shot of rum. I couldn't give up everything that gave life meaning. I ate what I wanted from fish to burgers. When I needed beer, I took the little boat over to Boca Grande and walked a few blocks to get another case. I gassed up while I was there.

I rigged up a method for charging the trolling motor battery from the big boat generator. I made a long run one day to Eldred's Marina on the mainland to buy more lures and assorted tackle. I stopped in the Waterside Grill at Gasparilla Marina for some conch fritters. I swung by the old Fishery on the way back and was surprised to see that it was gone. Nothing remained of the old restaurant or village. It had all been leveled for God knows what new development. That was one thing about Florida that bothered me. Landmarks that had been around for generations would disappear as soon as someone started waving condo money. This part of the state wasn't as bad as the east coast, but suburban creep was coming. Down at the tip of Gasparilla Island, a few hundred high-end homes were going up very close to the water's edge. They'd have their own beach, but the natural landscape would be scarred forever.

The old Mercury Motors testing facility had been torn down years ago. It probably wouldn't be long before someone built on that property. I always thought it would make a nice marina, but my financial situation wouldn't allow me to get a sniff at buying it, not that I wanted to take on such a project. I kept an eye on diesel tank levels in the Hatteras and considered my options for refueling. If all I wanted to do was get fuel, Burnt Store Marina was the best bet. If I wanted to combine the trip with getting supplies, Fort Myers Beach would work the best. Laishley Marina in Punta Gorda was an option, but it was a long walk to Publix. Palm Island Marina in Cape Haze was close, but that also involved a long walk to the grocery store.

I settled on Fort Myers Beach for two reasons. I could take the Redfisher for groceries. As long as I stopped in the restaurant at Snook Bight Marina, they'd let me use their dock. I could check to see if Captain Fred was back from Costa Rica. I was getting low of several things, but I wasn't quite ready to leave. My time alone had done me good. I was beginning to feel strong again. I was figuring out the fish. There was a little stretch of beach that was all mine every morning when I took my daily swim. I knew I had to go sooner or later, but I kept a close watch on my fuel and put it off as long as I could.

One morning very early, I was approached by a guy holding a cast net. He was just about to throw the thing at the waterline of my boat when I rushed out to stop him. I grabbed the handiest rifle and burst out into the cockpit.

"You hit my boat with that, and I'll put a hole in yours," I said.

Years back, I'd let a friendly fisherman throw his net at baitfish hiding in the shade of *Leap of Faith*. He'd asked permission first. He told me his name and offered to bring me milk or bread if I needed it. Once in a while, the lead weights on his net would smack the hull. I didn't mind much. The old boat was beat half to hell as it was. I didn't have the old boat anymore. I had a three million dollar Hatteras, and I knew what would happen if I let this guy throw his net near me.

"You don't own the water," he said.

"Maybe not," I said. "But I do own this gun. Is a half-dozen bait fish worth it?"

"Crazy bastard," he said, folding up his net.

"Good decision," I told him. "Don't come near this boat again or I'll open fire without a warning. You understand?"

"I got it," he said. "No need to be such an asshole."

"There's plenty of bait in the grass off that point over there," I said. "I've seen them there four days in a row."

"Thanks, I guess," he said. "I'll check it out."

I watched him, still holding my gun, as he used his trolling motor to move away and towards the grassy point. He wound up and threw his net. I could see he captured plenty of bait on his first throw. He gave me a thumbs up and left the area. I made a mental note of the brand of boat he was on, make and horsepower of his motor, and his physical description. I'd know if he came back.

Live bait was more effective at catching fish than lures here, but I could catch what I needed without it. One good fish would feed me for at least two days, and I didn't want to eat fish every single day. I still loved a good steak or a burger now and then. I had to force myself to add vegetables to the menu. Of course, beer and booze didn't help with fitness, but I swam and ran it off every morning. I was feeling lighter and faster than I ever felt in the mountains. I'd grown old there. My knees bothered me, and the aches multiplied in the cold weather. Here in the heat, I was mostly pain-free. My exercise regime was unhindered by the various physical ailments I'd experienced in the High Country.

I traded that for lots of sweat and the nightly mosquito raids. I quickly adjusted to being indoors with the air cranking as soon as the sun set. I thought it might be nice to have a grill to cook outdoors with before I was forced inside. I added it to the list. The list was getting longer and the fuel level was getting lower. As much as I hated to leave, I was going to have to go to town soon. I had trash to get rid of, and the holding tank needed to be pumped out. I couldn't put it off any longer.

I took my morning swim and jog before preparing to travel. I attached a long tow rope to the Redfisher and let it drift out behind the big boat. As I started to move across the bay, I ran down and shortened up the tow so that I could maneuver between the other anchored boats on my way out. I chose to run the Intracoastal south to Fort Myers Beach instead of going outside. I wasn't in a hurry to get there. One I got straightened up between the markers, I let my tow out a little further and settled in for the ride. I'd made this trip a hundred times before and it was my favorite piece of the coast. The incoming tide brought clear blue water in from the Gulf at each pass.

I marked off each island as I went by; North Captiva, Captiva, and Sanibel were all to starboard. Pine Island was off to port. I made a big sweeping left and went under the power-lines and into San Carlos Bay. I had always followed the shoreline of Sanibel and under the causeway to Fort Myers Beach, but the Hatteras was too tall. I had to go up the Caloosahatchee and through the Miserable Mile to fit under the tall bridge at Punta Rassa. Traffic was light, and I had no issues. Out from Punta Rassa, the Matanzas Pass markers became visible. The silly pirate ship from Salty Sam's Marina was on its way out with a boatload of kids.

I pulled my tow up close before entering the pass. I hailed the Pink Shell on the radio and was advised to take the same slip I'd been in prior. The tide was reaching full high, so the current was light, which made docking easy. The Redfisher bounced off the big boat a few times in the process, but I couldn't see any damage done to either boat. I spent the time to make sure each dock line was properly situated before hooking up to electric and water. I wouldn't need the generator, and I planned to get fuel on the way out like I'd done before.

I didn't see any signs of life on Captain Fred's boat. He would have come out to greet me if he was back in town. If he wasn't back in a few days, I'd miss him. It was my intention to take care of business and get the hell out of there as soon as possible. After one beer, I was ready to start working on my list. I asked the marina to pump out my holding tank at their earliest convenience, before taking the little boat to

Moss for gas. I filled up my extra cans while I was there. I dropped the cans off and started heading towards Publix.

I swung into the back bay, looking for Diver Dan and Robin. I found Robin and his little dog Kitty at home on his sailboat. He told me that Dan had a girlfriend on land and spent most of his time at her place, but he expected him back soon. We talked about Beth being back in town. Robin didn't seem overly pleased by that development, but I didn't get into it.

"I'll be around for two or three days," I said. "I've got a fancy new yacht over at Pink Shell."

"No shit," Robin said. "What are you living on now?"

"A fifty-four Hatteras," I said. "Sportfisher."

"Damn, man," he said. "Moving up in the world."

"It's a long story," I said. "Swing by later, and I'll fill you in. Tell Dan I said hi. I gotta go get some groceries."

"You have to go in the restaurant and buy something," he said. "They've been getting strict about that lately."

"I could eat," I said.

"Nice little flats boat too," he said. "You back to running coke or what?"

"No, man," I said. "It's all legit. Friends in high places."

"And here you are talking to your old friend in low places."

"I know it's been too long," I said. "But I didn't forget you guys."

"We figured you went and bought a house or something," he said. "It's been over a year."

"I did buy a house," I said. "Some bad shit went down, and now I'm back to my old tricks."

"Staying up in Pelican?"

"Yea, I'm here to restock and get fuel and whatnot," I said. "Doing my best to avoid people, other than you that is."

"If I see Dan I'll round him up and bring him over later," he said.

"Great," I said. "See you then."

I pulled up to the Bayfront Bistro within Snook Bight Marina and tied off to their dock. I went inside and took a seat at the bar. I asked for a beer and a menu. This was not a place I frequented. It was on the expensive side and not very welcoming to boat bums. I had always taken my dinghy up a canal to Topps Market for groceries. You had to deal with a much lower class of people there, and it was sometimes trouble, but it had suited my station in life at the time. It had since been torn down too. I ordered grouper strips, which was an appetizer. The bartender hesitated as if I'd also order an entrée.

"Have I ordered enough to get to Publix?" I asked.

"Sure, man," he said. "Just make it quick."

The grocery store shared a parking lot with the marina. You could push a cart fairly close to the dock and unload quickly. The carts had to be returned or someone would come out and yell at you. Over at Topps we just left the cart by the dock for the next person.

I loaded a cart full of meat and necessities, paid in cash, and pushed my cart as close as I could get it to the boat. I carried enough bags on each arm to qualify for the Olympics in weightlifting. I got my stuff situated in the boat and ran back to return the cart. I could feel the eyes on me. I was looked down upon by both the restaurant and marina staff, even though I was well dressed and clean-shaven. The Redfisher was expensive for its size. They were used to the grubby folks from the back bay or the mooring field. They would treat me differently if I came in on the Hatteras.

I considered checking their ship's store for a marine grill, but leaving was more important. Screw that snobby place. They didn't need any more of my money. I took the groceries back to the big boat and put everything away. I'd forgotten a few items, like bug spray, but I'd get them elsewhere or do without. I grabbed another beer and revisited my list. I had enough lures to last a while, but I could always run back to Eldred's for more when necessary. I could certainly make do without a grill. Where the hell was I going to find gun oil on this island? I'd never seen a gun shop in my travels here, and I'd been almost everywhere. I needed to make a quick Google search, but of course, I had no devices or connectivity. I remembered a computer for customer use at the Matanzas Inn office. They ran a hotel but also the mooring field. Procedures were pretty loose. I decided to attempt to gain internet access there.

It was a short walk from the Pink Shell. I walked in and acted like I belonged there. I typed in "Gun Shop Near Me" and presto; there was one on the water just a few miles away. It was at the end of a canal on the mainland, but very close to San Carlos Island. I clicked out of my search and split before anyone could question me. I went back and hopped in the flats boat and made a beeline for the gun shop. I found my gun oil and some extra ammo for the pistol that I'd bought in Panama. Instead of going straight back to the big boat, I instead tied up under the bridge with all the mooring field dinghies. They used to have a book exchange in the laundry room. My flats boat was too big for the limited docking space, but I'd only be a few minutes.

I selected a half-dozen thrillers from the cruiser's library and vacated the premises quickly. I was not a paying customer and technically shouldn't be taking books. I told myself I'd bring these back on my next visit. I untied my little boat and started cruising slowly back to the Pink Shell. Some inner signal alerted me to danger. I scanned all around looking for any potential source. I slowed down long before I reached my boat but within sight of it. There was a man sitting in the fighting chair on the back of *Miss Six*. It was Jim Starr. I spun the boat around quickly and headed back the way I came. I didn't think he saw me. He couldn't know about the Redfisher, but what was I supposed to do now?

I doubted he was there to pay me a friendly visit. He was pissed that I'd dumped him in Key West and he knew about the cash. I knew that he had a gun. I'd seen the weapon and watched him use it to great effect. He was fast and accurate. I was unarmed at the moment. All of my weapons were locked inside the Hatteras. If I boarded and faced him down with no weapon, it probably wouldn't go well for me. He didn't come all this way just to say hello. He came for the money and to get even with me; not just for ditching him, but for taking his boat.

I went back under the bridge at idle speed, trying to think of a plan. He'd expect me to come down the dock and he'd be ready with his gun. He wouldn't immediately shoot me because he wanted the money. If he had been able to break into the boat, he would have waited inside, not in the cockpit. Maybe he didn't even intend to kill me. He didn't seem to have that in him. He was there for the money, but he'd only shoot if forced to. That would create a big mess that neither of us wanted. I couldn't get the police involved. I had to stay invisible to law enforcement. That was the key to my long-term survival. If the cops responded to gunshots, he'd have trouble escaping with the money. He would use the gun to force me to surrender my cash, then leave with what he could get.

I'd dispersed and hidden the money in twenty different places all over the boat. I could hope for an opportunity to turn the tables on him while I was collecting it, but his skill with a pistol discouraged me from that idea. He had the drop on me. I needed to turn the odds back in my favor somehow. I idled on into the mooring field; working the problem through in my head. I needed help. I needed some manpower on my team to increase my odds of success. I sped up and steered for the back bay once again, hoping Robin was still on his boat and maybe even that Diver Dan was back.

Both of their boats had a skiff tied off to it. They were both at home. I couldn't guess how they would react to my request, but I had to ask. I went to Robin first.

"I need help with a dangerous situation," I said. "Guy on my boat, likely armed."

"You been here one damn day," Robin said. "What the fuck?"

"No time to explain," I said. "But I need you two as a distraction. I'll make the move myself."

"What move?"

"Let's get Dan first so I can explain it once," I said. "You in?"

"Shit," he said. "I guess I am. You need to check Dan's sobriety before enlisting him, though."

"Let's go."

Robin jumped on with me. I noticed his ever-present dive knife strapped to his leg. We motored over to Dan's boat and pulled up alongside.

"I'm seeing a ghost," Dan said. "Son of a bitch if it ain't Breeze."

"I'm sorry about this," I said. "But Robin and I are on our way to face down a man with a gun. You're welcome to join us."

"Isn't that a fine hello," he said. "One of these days you should stop by just to shoot the shit. Maybe have a couple beers."

"I'm back in the area, and I promise I'll do that," I said. "But right now I have a more pressing matter. What do you think?"

"You might consider giving me some details," he said. "For starters."

"I'm here on an expensive yacht," I began. "I had to repo it from its previous captain to get it. I've got a butt load of cash onboard that this man knows about. I ditched his ass in Key West, but he knew where I was headed. He's here to rob me and maybe get a little revenge."

"Is that all?" Dan asked. "Sounds like a walk in the park to me."

"I know I'm out of bounds here," I said. "But you know I'll do right by you."

"What is it exactly that you want us to do?" he asked.

"There will be three of us," I said. "But you two go in first. Tell him he's trespassing or whatever. I need you to board the boat and make a little fuss. Distract him so I can get on from the bow without him knowing. Rock the boat a little. I'll sneak up and jump him before he knows I'm there. You'll be there in case that goes wrong."

"And he's got a gun," Robin said.

"I know that he owns one," I said. "I have to assume he's holding it in his lap right now, but he doesn't want to shoot if he doesn't have to. That will bring the cops."

"What's your measure of this man?" Dan asked.

"He's not a badass," I said. "But he is good with that gun. If I can disarm him, he's not going to hurt any of us."

"What's this man want from you, Breeze?" asked Dan. "Revenge for some wrong you've done him?"

"He wants money," I said. "He's a grifter, and he knows I've got a bunch of cash. He helped me recover it. I paid him what we agreed, but he sees a shot at the whole pile."

"Say you do disarm him," Robin asked. "We got him tied up or whatever. What do we do with him after that?"

"That's an excellent question," I responded. "I'm open to ideas."

"Are you ready to roll out of here once he's taken care of?" Dan asked.

"I just need diesel," I said.

"Diversified closes at five," he said. "Moss is open until six. You'll be pushing it."

"I can't say that it will go down that fast," I said. "But I'm near empty. I can't leave without fuel."

EIGHTEEN

I could see that they intended to help. I just needed to give them a clear plan of attack. Diver Dan was older than me, but he'd seen plenty in his time. Nothing scared him much. Robin was young, wiry, and a bit high strung, but I knew that he was capable when the shit hit the fan.

"Let me ask a stupid question before we all jump this guy," Dan said. "Is there any particular reason we can't simply call the cops?"

"I can't involve the police," I said. "Let's just say that I need to stay incognito."

"That's that name of that big Hatteras that's always down at the Pink Shell," Robin said.

"There's two of them now," I said. "Mine is directly next to the one you always see. It's also named *Incognito VI*."

"Okay, no cops," Dan said. "But I'd like to hear that story sometime.

"I'll fill you in as soon as I can after this is over," I said. "You two take one of your boats. We'll all tie up under the bridge and walk from there. I'll lag back at the resort while you board and start harassing him. Make sure to move around, so he doesn't feel me climb on. Keep him distracted until I make my move."

They both nodded in agreement, and we left in separate boats to enact our plan to dislodge Starr and make him sorry he ever showed up. I didn't want to kill him, but I wouldn't lose sleep if he got hurt in the process. It needed to be clear to him that coming after me again would be a stupid thing to do.

There were only a few boats tied up at the dinghy dock, so there was room for both of our vessels. It was a short walk to the Pink Shell. I worked myself up on the way. The intruder intended to do me harm. That was his mistake. I peeled off from the other two before we could be seen from my boat.

"Be careful," I said. "I'm right behind you."

Dan and Robin strode down the dock with confidence. I watched first Robin and then Dan jump up on the gunnel and start yelling at Starr. Dan moved to the other side of the cockpit, which was my cue to board. I climbed onto the bow and scrambled up over the windshield and onto the bridge.

"This ain't your boat, asshole," Robin said.

"You're trespassing," Dan said. "I'm asking you nicely to leave right now."

"This six-shooter says you're the one's trespassing," Starr said. "Now beat it."

I was directly above Starr, who still sat in the fighting chair. He was pointing his pistol alternately at Dan and Robin. The jump down was further than I'd realized. This was going to hurt. It would help if Starr was standing, but I couldn't wait for the perfect moment. Dan glanced my way, and I motioned for him to get Starr to stand up.

"Put that piece down, and we can settle this like men," he said.

"I can put a hole in you before you make a fist," Starr said, beginning to stand up.

It was now or never. I jumped off the back of the bridge with my feet aimed at his shoulders. I hit him awkwardly, but it was more than enough to knock him down. The gun flew across the cockpit. I crashed into the rail next to

Dan, who partially broke my fall. I got a solid lump on my head and a severely jammed ankle. If I pulled that stunt alone, Starr could have easily overpowered me at that point, but Robin had the gun on him. Dan gave him a swift kick in the ribs for good measure. It was over that fast.

"You all right, Breeze?" Robin asked.

"There's some thin line in that compartment right behind you," I said. "Let's get his hands and feet bound."

Robin handed the weapon to Dan and pulled out the rope.

"I'll have him trussed up like a Christmas Turkey in thirty seconds," he said. "Leave the knot tying to a sailor."

I was still trying to clear the cobwebs in my head. Dan helped me up and sat me in the fighting chair. I felt like a king on his throne, other than my aching head and damaged ankle.

"You sure you're going to be all right?" Dan asked.

"Better than him," I said. "Run down and bring my flats boat back here."

Starr's feet and hands were tied snuggly. He looked up at me from the deck.

"I just wanted the money," he said. "I wasn't going to hurt anyone or take the boat."

"We're not going to kill you, dumb fuck," I said. "But it looks like I'll be keeping the money and the boat. You lose."

"What are you going to do to me?"

"Nothing," I said. "We're going to let you go free, but if you ever try me again, I'll see that you're dead. Do we have an understanding?"

He nodded in agreement.

"Not that your word is good for anything," I said.

Dan pulled up with the Redfisher. I tried to help get Starr over the gunnel and into the flats boat, but my ankle had other ideas. Dan came to my rescue, and I watched as the bound man was plopped onto the foredeck of the little boat.

"Have we decided where to drop him?" I asked.

"We figured Picnic Island," Dan said. "Someone will be by tomorrow or the next day. He can beg a ride to the mainland."

"How far is it from here?" I asked.

"Five miles, give or take," Robin said. "Get your fuel quick. We'll be back shortly."

"I'll meet you at Moss," I said. "I've got a little something to give each of you."

They took off to release the captive on an uninhabited island that the locals used to party. In the worst-case scenario, he'd have to wait until the weekend to get picked up. It was more likely that someone would rescue him the very next day. One night swatting mosquitoes and sleeping outdoors wouldn't kill him.

I hobbled around untying lines while the engines warmed up. My ankle was swelling by the minute. I needed to ice it down, but that would have to wait. The lump on my head had grown too, but I'd taken harder hits to the noggin. I backed out into the channel and swung the boat around. The outer fuel dock was open, so I pulled right up to it with ease. While the attendant stayed with the hose, I ducked inside to grab a bag of cash. I used some of it to pay the bill. I counted out ten grand to give to my backwater friends. They weren't suffering from extreme poverty. I knew they could take care of themselves, but a little bonus would be nice.

It takes a good while for a thousand gallons of fuel to flow. Dan and Robin were back before my tanks were full. They helped me rig up the tow line for the Redfisher, and I handed Dan the stack of bills.

"Split that up evenly," I said. "Buy me a beer when I get back here."

"Come back there and anchor with us when you do," Robin said. "That fancy marina brought you nothing but trouble."

"You're right about that," I said. "I was hoping to catch Captain Fred there. Maybe next time."

"You still owe us a story," Dan said. "It ought to be a good one."

"Did you keep the guy's revolver?" I asked.

"Dropped in the deep water under the bridge," Robin said.

"How did your captive like his new digs?"

"He didn't seem impressed," Dan said. "Ungrateful fellow."

"We had to be a little rough with him," Robin said. "He chose not to cooperate there at the end, but he'll survive."

"All the better," I said. "I was afraid he was getting off too easy."

We said our goodbyes and I eased away from the fuel dock. I hoped that every trip back to society wouldn't go like this one had. I should pick a different town next time, but I needed to meet up with Captain Fred. I shelved that worry for another time. I had enough supplies to last a month or more. I could always call him with the SAT phone.

I chose the Gulf route for the return trip to Pelican Bay. *Miss Six* hummed along with her little brother in tow. It was late in the day. I slowed down to watch the sun sink into the water. It was a glorious moment. I wished that Brody could have been there to see it.

I thought about all that had happened in such a short time. I had given myself to the High Country just over one year ago. I'd done my best to become a mountain man. There were times when I was one with the wilderness, but those times seemed far behind me. I'd taken a strange coastal route to a new beginning. It started with coastal Carolina, twisted south through Florida to the west coast of Panama and the east coast of Colombia. From there, I stopped in Belize, Mexico, and Cuba. I made a fast pit stop in Key West and finally returned to Cayo Costa, the Coastal Key.

I am no longer Mountain Breeze. Now, I am Coastal Breeze. It's good to be back.

Author's Thoughts

Jim Starr contacted me about using his name for a character in one of my books. He told me he was a mechanic, that he played the guitar, and that he smoked and drank too much. I hope that he enjoys his fictional self. If you would like to see your name in a Breeze adventure, send me an email at: **Kimandedrobinson@gmail.com**

Breeze was created in Southwest Florida and enjoyed a long run as a loveable boat bum anti-hero before moving to the mountains of western North Carolina. My wife and I spent a year in a log cabin in the woods there, so I brought the character along in the **Mountain Breeze Series**. We decided that we weren't really mountain people, so we moved to the coast, hence the change in Breeze's direction. If this is your first encounter with Breeze, I urge you to investigate the **Trawler Trash Series**, which I'll link to in the following pages.

Please don't send me political vitriol because I suggested that the FBI might be involved in a murderous plot. It's fiction folks. Half the thrillers I've ever read involve some government agency going rogue. Maybe Jim Starr will run into Jeffrey Epstein on Picnic Island?

Diver Dan and Robin are actual friends of mine who live on boats in Fort Myers Beach. I've been out of touch since leaving Florida, but this work serves to let them know I still think of them. One-legged Beth is also a real person. All three of these friends are used fictitiously.

Petey's Upper Deck at the Matanzas Inn is bayside at Fort Myers Beach. They have the best pizza in town, and you can catch Scott Bryan on Monday evenings from five to nine. Look for the Leap of Faith sticker on his guitar.

https://matanzasonthebay.com/peteys-upper-deck/

https://www.facebook.com/scotty.bryan66

Sign up for my email list for new release information and special offers:

https://mailchi.mp/6ca0c23d88dc/signup

THE TRAWLER TRASH SERIES

ALSO STARRING BREEZE

Trawler Trash; Confessions of a Boat Bum
https://amzn.to/2JqXFNJ

Following Breeze
https://amzn.to/2JNjM0k

Free Breeze
https://amzn.to/2LQZQMD

Redeeming Breeze
https://amzn.to/2JPmLVO

Bahama Breeze
https://amzn.to/2JusIbl

Cool Breeze
https://amzn.to/2JusIbl

True Breeze
https://amzn.to/2JQHUyT

Ominous Breeze
https://amzn.to/2EhHzSu

Restless Breeze
https://amzn.to/2w9P5Ks

Enduring Breeze
https://amzn.to/2HHktW6

Benevolent Breeze
https://amzn.to/2VPXSR9

THE MOUNTAIN BREEZE SERIES

Banner Elk Breeze
https://amzn.to/2NgGa3E

Blue Ridge Breeze
https://amzn.to/2N97i4M

Beech Mountain Breeze
https://amzn.to/30dLQiS

High Country Breeze
https://amzn.to/2HDH45T

New River Breeze
https://amzn.to/2TNyAz7

NON-FICTION BOOKS BY ED ROBINSON

Leap of Faith; Quit Your Job and Live on a Boat
http://amzn.to/1bwkvxu

Poop, Booze, and Bikinis
http://amzn.to/1g7du7q

The Untold Story of Kim
http://amzn.to/1kuJqFr

Acknowledgements

Proofreaders:
Dave Calhoun
Jeanene Olson
Don Nobles

Editor:
John Corbin

Cover Design:
https://ebooklaunch.com/

Interior Formatting:
https://ebooklaunch.com/

Made in United States
Orlando, FL
29 February 2024

44220140R00173